LUNA STATION
QUARTERLY

Issue 050 | June 2022

Editor-in-Chief

Jennifer Lyn Parsons

Editors

Katrina Carruth • Anna Catalano • Wanda Evans
Angelica Fyfe • Cathrin Hagey • Sarah Pauling • Cait Ryan
Carly Racklin • Shana Ross • Gô Shoemake
Bridget Siniakov • Margaret Stewart • Izzy Varju

LUNA STATION PRESS
NEW JERSEY

First Paperback Edition June 2022
ISBN: 978-1-949077-33-9

Luna Station Quarterly publishes short fiction on March 1st, June 1st,
September 1st, and December 1st. For more information and submission
guidelines, please visit our website at lunastationquarterly.com

For Luna Station Press

Creative Director - Tara Quinn Lindsey
Editor-in-Chief & Founder - Jennifer Lyn Parsons

www.lunastationpress.com

CONTENTS

Editorial

Jennifer Lyn Parsons

Jennifer Lyn Parsons is a writer and senior software engineer. Currently, she enjoys writing fantasy stories about middle-aged people who aren't into the whole "going on a quest" thing but do it anyway. When not writing code or prose, she is also the editor-in-chief of the venerable Luna Station Quarterly. She finds joy in baseball, tea, discovering music new and old, and making analog things.

When I started Luna Station Quarterly, I didn't really have a plan for it. I knew I wanted to see more of the kinds of stories my friends and I were writing out in the world. I knew I had the skills to build a website and organize a magazine. Beyond that, I didn't know what running a magazine like LSQ was going to look like.

This lack of foresight was an advantage in my case. It enabled me, and by extension LSQ, to be flexible. The format could change, the design could change, how many people I had on staff could change. And change it did, quite often in fact. The development and growth of LSQ was an iterative process, and I'm grateful for my past self's naive approach because it has grown and evolved well beyond anything I could have imagined back in 2009.

With all that behind me, I find myself sitting here writing the editorial for issue 050. What an incredible milestone. So much, almost everything really, is different. We publish print editions thanks to new print-on-demand technology. We've seen the rise of ebook readers and the stabilization of that format that, it turns out, was not the death knell of print. The issue of LSQ that you hold in your hands, or visit on our website, looks completely different from that sweet little website I launched all those years ago, it's theme and layout I coded by hand now long forgotten.

Because so much is different, I decided to do something with this issue that brings things back around to the beginning. I wanted to do something that would tie this fiftieth issue to that first one. As such, you may have noticed that the artwork on the cover of this issue is in black and white.

When LSQ began publishing, print-on-demand publishing didn't exist yet in any reasonable, useful way for a magazine like this. Still, I wanted a way for those who preferred reading offline to have that option available. Print zines of all kinds were still quietly flourishing at the time and I was very much (and still am) attracted to the grassroots accessibility of printing something you made at your local copy store.

To support that intention, and because LSQ felt very much like a zine to me back in those early days, the first couple of years we published a printer-friendly PDF of every issue.

As a nod to those early issues, issue 050 has a black and white cover, with much thanks to Theodora Capat for the gorgeous illustration. Though this time I wouldn't suggest printing your own copy. At almost 300 pages, it would be a bit of a bear! I always wondered if anyone ever printed out those early issues for their collections.

There's one thing that definitely hasn't changed, and it's honestly the best part. From issue 001 to 050, every issue is consistently packed with a collection of amazing stories. The one you're reading now is no exception. I'm consistently amazed by the variety we receive in our slush pile every quarter. Narrowing those tales down to the final choices is both my favorite part of the job and the hardest. Thank you, as always, to our hard-working editors who help me manage this challenge!

Now, send you on your way with a quote from my very first editorial:

Genre fiction, in particular, can do extraordinary things. When grounded to a solid character or idea, the lessons of the ages can be passed from author to reader. Profound experiences are shared in the deepest ways, in the poetry of words, the explora-tion of the mind, and the opening of the heart.

And that is the kind of story I hope to share with you. A little action and adventure, a few surprises, twists, and turns, wouldn't be too bad either, and you'll find those within these pages as well.

I do hope you enjoy the stories we're presenting this first issue. Each of the authors within have contributed something special and all their own. I'm so thrilled to be able to share them with you.

L S Q | 050

Tatterdemalion, or of Apple Bough and Straw

Elou Carroll

Elou Carroll likes to tell ghost stories and make up fairy tales. She haunts Twitter at @keychild, and keeps a catalogue of her weird little wordcreatures on www. eloucarroll.com.

On a little farm, up a little hill, not far from a little village, a farmer's wife was wailing. So long had she cried for her husband that the crows and the ravens and the jackdaws had eaten up her plaintive notes and scattered them like seeds down the little hill, and dropped them like pennies across the little village.

The baker sent fresh bread but the farmer's wife did not eat. The wisewoman left tea upon her stoop but the farmer's wife did not drink. She tended the animals and crops as she ought but could take no pleasure. When she tried to read, the ink slipped from the pages and pooled in her palms. Every song she sang turned to one long, mournful cry upon her tongue. Everything the farmer's wife tried, grew cold and brittle and cracked between her fingers.

And so, instead, she walked.

The farmer's wife walked from the old stone farmhouse, through the creaking wooden barn, and up to the top of the little hill where an apple tree was waiting. The apple tree was a crooked thing and had stood upon the hill longer by far than the farm. It had been her husband's favorite.

Not so long ago, a cruel wind swept through the little village, up the little hill and in through the door of the farmhouse—which had always been swinging to and fro with villagers and their children, farm cats and their kittens, and the odd strange little visitor from the woods nearby. It brought with it a fever and, before it went, scooped her husband up and carried him far away.

She buried him beneath the apple tree.

The farmer's wife cried for so long, and so deeply, that the ground of his grave grew thick with grass and the apple tree flourished—heavy with red, red apples.

Before long the crows and the ravens and the jackdaws forgot the cadence of her wailing, the baker stopped leaving bread and the wisewoman tea, and the farmer's wife's eyes were dry but her heart, which had been so full for so, so long, remained empty.

***

When Summer lifted her skirts and tiptoed down the little hill and through the little village with Autumn close at her heels, it came time to harvest.

But the farmer's wife was old and the cattle that worked the farm had always been her husband's creatures. No matter how hard she pushed or how nicely she spoke to them, the cows refused to work.

"Come on, you great, lumbering milk-sacks." The farmer's wife heaved the reins but Felicity—the farmer's once-prized cow—would not budge.

There was a skittering from the wall, and when she turned her head, a crow pattered towards her. "Need help?"

"No, little crow. I just wish my husband were here."

"You should call on the wiswoad." It cawed.

The farmer's wife frowned. "The what-what?"

"The wiswoad. In the woods, small fellow, big feet and a long nose. You can't miss it." The crow cocked its head. "The wiswoad can help. Take a gift, make a wish."

"Well, we'll see about that." With one last tug on Felicity's reins—"Stupid thing!"—the farmer's wife sighed and huffed and stomped back to the farmhouse. She bustled around the kitchen and rustled together a basket of bread and cured meats, cheese and butter, apples and freshly baked biscuits. The farmer's wife slung her shawl across her shoulders and trudged down the little dirt track to the woods.

The trees reached out in welcome, brushed her shoulders and ushered her along. The woods had changed since her youth; the trees were no longer uptight things with straight trunks and uniform branches, standing in regimental rows—now, they leant and bent and whirled in circles, the whorls of their knots peering back at her like round, black eyes. Their roots bridged up from the ground and made messy pathways across the stamped earth.

The farmer's wife wobbled down the trail. It wound around between the oak, the chestnut, the ash and the elder, but never did it split. The path shot straight through the wood, on and on until it met a small house, with a small stream beside it.

From one fungiform chimney puffed clouds of pale purple smoke, up and up until it drifted into the great pregnant belly of the clouds. The little red door was open just slightly and the scent of a wood fire wafted out of it, infused with lavender and herbs that the farmer's wife couldn't place.

The farmer's wife cleared her throat. When nothing happened, she crouched—her old bones creaking like the barn door's hinges—and knocked one knuckle on the tiny door.

"What?" came a voice. "What is it? I'm busy. Busy, busy!"

"Are..." croaked the farmer's wife, and coughed. "Are you the wiswoad?"

One large lilac eye peered out from the gap between the door and the frame. "Might be." It looked her up and down. "Very might be."

As the door swung open, the farmer's wife hobbled backwards, and the little creature stepped out. It wore a purple hat on its little head and purple boots on its big feet and a coat of deep maroon. The wiswoad tilted its head in greeting and its long nose nearly grazed the ground.

"I've brought you a gift," said the farmer's wife, shifting the basket across the ground with her foot.

"Gift, gift." The wiswoad rifled through the basket—when it got to the cheese, it scrunched its nose up and gagged deep in its throat. The wiswoad grabbed the offending parcel and lobbed it into the stream. It leant back on its haunches then and smiled a sharp-toothed smile. "Good, good."

The wiswoad sat on a little stump and spread its hands. "A favor for a friend?"

"I..." The farmer's wife wrung her hands and chewed her bottom lip. "I'm struggling on the farm. I'm old and exhausted and have no sons to tend it for me. The animals and I...we never got on. We should all like my husband back—please."

"A very big favor." The creature tipped its hat back and peered up at the farmer's wife.

"A very big basket," she retorted.

The wiswoad tapped its lips and considered her, a slow smile crept across its lips and a twinkle glittered in its eye. It left a long finger on its chin and nodded. "Okay. Done. Basket, husband, deal."

"How?" asked the farmer's wife.

"Cut down branch of once-favorite tree, bury it beneath straw, leave clothes and close door. Sleep night through and husband be waiting for you." With that, the wiswoad tugged the basket towards its little house and pulled it through the little door with a crunch—the door being far smaller than the basket, though the wiswoad didn't seem to mind.

Later, the farmer's wife took a hatchet to the apple bough above her husband's grave and hefted it across to the barn. She left it beneath the straw as the wiswoad bade and on top she laid his favorite shirt, trousers, boots and hat—she even left a square for his pocket, a little paisley pattern made from one of her skirts.

Before she left, she kissed her fingertips and placed them where his heart would be.

***

That night, when the wiswoad winked its great purple eye through a knot-hole in the barn's wall, the straw began to shuffle. The farmer's shirt slipped between the wisps, followed by his trousers and then his boots.

A cool breeze swept past and the apple bough stood, clothes hanging loosely on its form; the breeze circled around and carried some of the straw up with it, which barrelled beneath the shirt and up the legs of the trousers. Soon, the bough became a man and the man collected his hat from the floor and popped it on his head.

First he looked like a scarecrow—nothing more than a rickety old tatterdemalion—but as the wiswoad watched, the farmer came to life.

Outside, a small root buckled and the plant above it drooped, fell, died.

***

There was a cockerel in the window and it was screeching.

The farmer's wife leapt up and the bird batted its wings and screamed past her, its little talons catching in her hair. "Away with you, you foul thing!"

She grunted, her old bones protesting the early hour.

The farmer's wife went about her morning, near-sure she'd dreamt the crow and the woods and the wiswoad. Even when she noticed her largest basket was missing, she couldn't quite bring herself to believe in the adventure of the day before.

She lumbered past the open barn door, and greeted her husband. *Greeted her husband?*—the farmer's wife stopped then, dropped the firewood she carried, and rushed back to the barn.

There he was, feeding each cow in turn, scratching behind their ears and telling jokes to a chorus of mooing, just as he used to. He greeted the goats next, tickled their chins and murmured into their long ears how he'd missed them.

"Arthur?" whispered the farmer's wife with a hand on her heart and a quiver in her voice.

"There you are, my pet. I was just telling Felicity what a wonderful sleep I had last night." He opened his arms and the farmer's wife folded herself into them.

"Oh, Arthur!" she sobbed and while she sobbed, she didn't notice the cows behind them sagging, their bellows growing low.

The farmer worked the farm and his wife watched. She watched the way his arms moved, the way the breeze swept through his hair, the tilted shuffle of his gait. She tried not to notice the crops withering behind him.

It's normal, she thought when Felicity struggled to pull the plough. *It's a difficult task. She's just tired.*

And when the farm cat was unable to climb the low wall around her herb garden, she told herself, *She's old, not as spry as she once was.* Though she knew the cat had been but a kitten the summer before last. Without Arthur to help, she'd hand reared the little thing herself.

But when husband and wife walked up the little hill and looked out over the little village, apples dropped rotten from her husband's favorite tree. They landed deep in the pit of her stomach.

Each moment spent with Arthur, the more she shook with the effort. Her arms were logs and her legs great trunks, each of them dragging heavy, as if laying roots. When they reached the door of the farmhouse, and the farmer's wife was wheezing, her husband kissed her hand, bid her goodnight and started back to the barn.

"Arthur?" She frowned.

"There's more work to be done, my pet. You go on." The farmer looked over his shoulder and tipped his hat in the same way he had every morning, when he left for the fields or the barn or the market. As the grasses and shrubs blackened at his passing, tears stung his wife's eyes and the breath died in her throat.

***

The way through the woods was wilder than it had been before and the farmer's wife was tired, so tired. Every move was as if made through mud, thick and cloying, and hardening with each step.

The closer she got to the wiswoad, the more her exhaustion faded. Further away from her husband, the air became lighter and brighter were the leaves. Her chest might have loosened, her breath might have come smoother but the farmer's wife did not notice. Instead, there was a burning in her diaphragm, her throat, on her tongue, in her veins.

"Get out here, you tricksy little imp!"

Something rustled in the undergrowth. Then the wiswoad appeared, chewing on an air-hardened crust.

"What?" It said, spraying breadcrumbs across the path.

"You tricked me."

"No trick. You ask for life, life takes life. Husband lives so others must sicken, others, maybe wife, must die." The wiswoad picked at its long nails.

The farmer's wife shook, she bit her tongue for a moment, clenched and unclenched her fists. "You failed to mention that. You said a gift for a husband."

"You did not ask." The creature sucked its teeth. "Cannot answer unasked questions."

"Well, you need to fix it. Fix him. Fix the farm."

It sighed and sung, "Only wife can fix."

Sucking air between her teeth, the farmer's wife kicked the ground. "How exactly?"

"What's dead must die, must be left to lie, and what's alive will thrive..." It smiled a curled smile. "And survive."

Her shoulders sagged. "You—you want me to kill..."

The wiswoad shrugged its small shoulders, clicked its tongue.

Sobs struggled out from between her lips and her fingers were there to catch them. The farmer's wife collected her cries in her palms, then held them over her chest, and let go. When she opened her eyes, the wiswoad was gone.

***

The farm grew weary from the hill like an abandoned seed husk, mottled and dark and rotting. The animals, so beloved by her once-husband, were huddled and weak. Down the hill, the fields were cracked and dying, and there was the farmer tending them though there was nothing left to tend.

Straw poked from between his teeth, he whistled and walked with a grin on his face and a spring in his step. An ache tremored where her heart should have been and the back of her throat burned.

"Just straw and wood," she whispered.

The closer she got to her husband, the heavier her eyelids became, the more she shook, ached, and the more her heart fell to her stomach, heavy like a clod of earth.

When she reached him, he opened his arms but the farmer's wife shook her head. She turned from him and hobbled further up the hillside. He followed, as she knew he would.

"Just straw and wood."

The apple tree stood dead in front. In its branches sat the crow, whose feathers had dulled and fallen as if it were a tree making way for winter. As they approached—the farmer's wife and her straw husband—it let out a mournful caw and swept clumsily away.

"Fetch me an apple, would you?" asked the farmer's wife, barely more than a whisper.

"Anything for you, my pet," came her husband's reply.

And he turned, and he stretched—

And as her life slipped between the lines of her skin and her breath grew raspy and short, the farmer's wife struck the flint she carried always in her apron and set her straw husband aflame.

***

After the fire, when there was nothing left of her husband or the tree, the farmer's wife swept the ash from her true-husband's grave. Beneath the remnants of straw and bough, there sat an apple—deep red and perfect. She picked it up, warm like a heart, and closed her eyes.

Down the hill, the farm was lush and green.

And alive.

Osteomancy

Jenna Grieve

Jenna Grieve is a writer from Scotland. She likes to write literary short fiction with a splash of magic. Her work has also appeared in Firewords magazine.

Stranger presented his own humerus to Locksmith with his remaining hand.

"Please. Will you make me a key?"

If the amputation had been intended, then Stranger—or the surgeon hired—had performed dismally. Black blood pooled and congealed at the bulbous remains of his shoulder, in the shape of a snake's forked tongue. What poisonous memories lay in that wound? Locksmith looked at the bone instead—the reason Stranger had sought him out. Stranger's humerus was the sort of bone one might casually toss a drooling stray dog. Scraps of rotting tissue hung at either end where it had once united with shoulder and elbow. Some attempt had been made to clean it, but stubborn blood stains dragged veiny grooves along its length. Stranger held only his humerus—where were the radius, ulna, and the countless bones in the hand and wrist? Trapezium. Capitate. Scaphoid. Lunate. Did these relics of Stranger breadcrumb his path to Locksmith, or were they stashed safe somewhere? Didn't he want to take them through the door?

Locksmith, hunched upon his windowsill, the shutter looming above him, shushed his stomach as it mewled like a hungry newborn. He might eat again, if this man could pay. Locksmith's gaze trailed slowly from the bone, up Stranger's skeleton-shrunk body, to his eyes. Peppercorn gray, they slouched with the kind of exhaustion which clung permanently to a person, the sort which gathered in un-washable layers like the sand. Locksmith had seen many heads bow in defeat after too many harsh decades. Maybe Stranger viewed the impending transaction as finally giving in. If Locksmith could heal his worries, make him see that the door might not be the best option...but no. As a rule, he didn't interfere.

"Please come in."

Locksmith swung his legs off the windowsill and cursed the pain in his foot as it took his weight for the first time in hours. When business was quiet—and it always was these days—there was nothing else to do but sit in that window frame, his perch overlooking it all. The town. The dunes. The door, obscured by the dunes, waiting with a sickly, impure, sort of hope. Locksmith had tracked Stranger's meandering path over the sand, had imagined someone above, perhaps whatever god cursed them all to this existence, playing with Stranger like a marionette, invisible strings garrotted around his three limbs. The midday sun loved to taunt one's sense of distance and balance. He'd wanted to help, but Locksmith also struggled on the sand, so he only watched, fancying himself some sort of guardian of the desert's lost souls. All the while, the shutter crouched above Locksmith, threatening, like a guillotine. It had never yet fallen of its own accord, but each night when he released it, it smacked down with such eagerness that he knew it must ache for that moment all day.

Locksmith lived near a lonesome village which every year sank a little further into sand. His workshop—once painted a powdery blue, now bleached by the desert—was the closest building to the bone door. Before he brought the shutter down, he gathered up all his empty teacups and transferred them to a table. Each one was broken in a different place, hairline cracks into which the sand still managed to bury. Locksmith always soaked his hunger with tea imbued with a squeeze of lemon, a swish of cinnamon, a sprig of mint, or a pod of cardamom. He liked to pretend these flavors counted as meals.

Stranger watched with little obvious emotion and clutched his humerus awkwardly. Dust clouded angrily when the shutter hit. He limped to his door, allowed the man, and more sand, inside. Was the sand so invasive on the other side of the bone door?

Chairs screeched backwards. Locksmith brushed off most of the sand, which slumped to the floor with a lazy sigh. He offered tea and bread, but Stranger shook his head, softly, as if even this was too much effort. Perhaps Locksmith should offer him a bed, but Stranger was the first human he'd seen in a while. He needed this to last a little longer. And maybe, if Stranger liked it here with Locksmith, he'd abandon his plan to go through the door. Locksmith snapped the thickest finger of his aloe vera plant and gave it to Stranger, who squeezed it between his thumb and fore-finger and applied the juice to his wound as best he could with his right hand. Locksmith's thoughts barbed—he should have offered to do it for him. He ought to have offered boiled water first to cleanse it, then the aloe, then a bandage. But he had no bandages, and nothing he could do would be a miracle cure. Did miracle cures lie beyond the bone door?

There were no introductions. Locksmith no longer asked his cus-tomers their names. It made it more painful when they left him. Many volunteered the information anyway, but not Stranger. Locksmith threw a handful of common local names around in his head, holding them up against Stranger's dull complexion, and his unexpectedly kind eyes. Nothing fit him well. Locksmith shook himself—he'd been staring silently for too long.

"Rumors about you stretch throughout the desert...some of them are rather unkind." They were the first words Stranger had spoken since his request for a key. His voice was quiet and hoarse. Locksmith knew all too well how grains of sand could become lodged in the throat and erode away the delicate skin. Tea with honey would help him, and Locksmith regretted that he had used the last of his honey on his own selfish throat a fortnight ago.

"I know."

"Why do you do it?"

"Make keys? My mother taught me."

"Bone keys."

"My mother did not teach me that," Locksmith conceded. Stranger sipped his tea. He was a little younger than Locksmith himself, perhaps in his early forties, with a splattering of receding hair. Certainly old enough to have children and perhaps young enough to have parents. There must be people who would miss him. His skin was a little lighter than Locksmith's own, and a little greyer, shrouded with the same tired ache of his eyes. Perhaps he was ill. Was that why he wanted to go through the door? A dying man risking everything would be a compelling, if far from novel, motive for Stranger. Locksmith wasn't sure it fit this man. He wanted to open him up, dissect him.

"You aren't from this town," Locksmith observed. "Where are you from?"

"Far," Stranger said. "Nowhere's the same as it was." A shiver pushed his wounded shoulder, and Locksmith hoped it wasn't shock or trauma from loss of limb. He was no doctor, and Stranger would not be the first to die before they reached the door.

"Why do you wish to go through the door?" Locksmith asked it too early, the question he always wanted them to answer.

Stranger shook his head and passed a hand over his dirt-strewn forehead. Locksmith waited, but no explanation came. Many people went through because they were convinced death lay on the other side. They were suicidal, or dying anyway, and wanted some control over the matter. Others followed loved ones, whether that be into death or not. Some bore a curiosity so strong they would pay whatever price necessary. Locksmith decided not to press Stranger for his reason, but there was something he felt he needed to say.

"I don't necessarily know if it's a good thing, going through the door. I don't know if what I do saves lives, ruins them, or ends them. I don't know if you are my victim or my patient."

Locksmith desperately needed the money. A few bone keys a year just about kept his belly lined with food, even if nobody wanted his normal keys. But he was never comfortable playing with lives like this. The door was the best and worst thing that had ever happened to him.

"You're not the one making the decision, just providing a service," Stranger said quietly. He ran a finger absently along the humerus in his lap. The statement didn't sit right with Locksmith. Stranger's arm twisted awkwardly to pull a coin pouch from his trouser pocket. "They told me what you charge. Tell me if it isn't right."

Locksmith hated asking for money. He'd count it later, when Stranger wasn't watching. He held the pouch tight to his chest.

He could live a little longer. Stranger's expression towards the bone shifted to repulsion, as if he was just noticing the rotting fragments of flesh. He offered it to Locksmith again, and Locksmith took it.

"What happens now?" Stranger asked.

"You don't need to do anything else, just relax here. I shall get started now, if you like." He stood, already regretting how the one conversation he'd had in weeks had stayed at surface level, how he could have said and done more to make Stranger more comfortable in what could be his final hours. Candlelight glinted in Stranger's gray eyes. "Stay a while," he murmured.

Locksmith sat back down far too fast, trying to control the smile that ached to stretch his face. He repeated his earlier offer of tea and bread, and this time Stranger accepted. It was Locksmith's last loaf, but he could buy more with the money from the key. He added lemon to the tea, hoping this might help soothe Stranger's throat, and then perhaps he'd be more talkative. He wanted to ask more questions, but he'd never been good at starting an interesting conversation. Both men finished their tea, then another cup, this time with clove, and sat in silence. It was Stranger who spoke first this time, much to Locksmith's delight.

"You know the door better than anyone. What do you think lies behind it?"

"Nobody knows." Locksmith's heart skipped. His customers always asked this, and Locksmith could never think of anything insightful or wise to tell them.

"You've watched others go through. What do you see when it opens?"

"Nothing. I've tried, but my eyes are blind to everything beyond the threshold."

"Because you have no key of your own?"

Locksmith hesitated. "Perhaps."

"But don't the people tell you what they see?"

Locksmith furrowed his brow. "They say they cannot. Eventually I stopped asking. These days, I leave the customer to go through on their own. It's their experience, not mine."

"Customer," Stranger repeated, his voice hollow. Locksmith balled up his tongue. What else could he call them?

"You can watch when I go through, if you like," Stranger said. "To satiate your curiosity."

Locksmith paused, then shook his head. The silence threatened a return, just for a second, before Stranger continued.

"You asked why I want to go through the door." Locksmith sat up so quickly his tea sloshed over the side and onto his trousers. He pinched his nose and glanced at the ceiling. Locksmith hoped it was dark enough that Stranger wouldn't notice the coven of cobwebs. He set his cup down on the sand-strewn floor and dabbed at his trousers with the scrunched corner of his shirt.

"I don't have to tell you, do I? It won't affect the key?"

Locksmith's heart sank. "Of course not. Everyone is entitled to their secrets."

He stared at Stranger, trying to imagine what sort of life he might have lived that led him here. The dying light outside shone on the hairs of his beard, revealing a blend of subtly different browns and grays where before Locksmith had believed there to be a monochrome. Stranger's eyes began to flicker closed, quickly at first, then sinking into a lethargic rhythm of open for four seconds, then closed for eight, over and over again. It dawned on Locksmith quite some time into his daydreaming that he was being rude in his staring. He flinched backwards and snatched up his half-spilled teacup. Stranger stirred at the sudden movement and Locksmith took a long gulp to hide his flushed cheeks.

"You should sleep," Locksmith said gently. "And I will craft your key."

***

It was Locksmith's own bed, but he didn't tell Stranger that. Locksmith brought him a fresh blanket and yet another cup of tea. Stranger sat on the bed and leaned back against the wall. A zig-zagging crack jutted into his head like a lightning strike. From this angle Stranger looked older, greyer, smaller, weaker. The finity of his time with Stranger struck Locksmith harder now the man was almost asleep. Tomorrow, he'd pass through the door, and he would always be a mere acquaintance to Locksmith. Stranger opened one eye and smiled up at him.

"I'll tell you my story, if you like," Locksmith said. It was the smile that made him do it. He cursed himself—Stranger wanted to sleep.

"About the door?" Stranger asked. Locksmith coughed, clearing the sand from his throat.

"Yes." He wrung his hands, and perched on the edge of the bed. He was reminded of his mother, tucking Locksmith and his sister to sleep with a story. "You see, I used to co-own this locksmithing business with my sister. And when the sand got more aggressive, and when the door appeared, everything changed."

Locksmith remembered the fear in everyone's eyes, the gossip which danced on everyone's lips, the flush of color in their cheeks as the world burned calmly. The door was either the cause of their misfortune or a beacon of hope—a way out. The people couldn't quite decide which.

"My sister became obsessed with the door. So did others, at first. But they lost curiosity when they realized the door could not be opened, and it became a generally ignored anomaly in the landscape. People turned their attention to the greater issue of the sand as it spread like a plague. But my sister, she convinced herself the door was meant for us, a puzzle to solve."

Stranger had closed his eyes again, but at Locksmith's mention of the sand, he brushed grains from his arms. Locksmith paused to do the same. Mere thought or mention of sand made his skin itch.

"She realized that the lock was made of bone, which propelled my sister to experiment. At first she tried animal bones: chickens and cows and donkeys. When they didn't work she would try a different animal, a different bone, a different method of shaping the key. Eventually she turned to humans—she'd visit hospitals and beg to purchase amputated limbs or bones from the newly-dead. Her keys flooded this workshop, hung on the walls, miniature dunes on every surface. She'd study them, comparing her iterations. Then one day I woke to find she'd worked through the night to fashion a key out of one of her own bones. The bone from her great toe: Hallux."

Stranger's eyes snapped open. He leaned towards Locksmith, baited by his tale.

"And that key worked?"

Locksmith bit his lip, remembering how he'd screamed at her when he saw what she'd done, his terror at the blood soaking through her clumsy knot of bandages. How calm but firm she was, telling him she needed to make a working key, that he didn't understand. That he wasn't a true locksmith if he didn't think this mystery was somehow theirs, if he didn't need answers.

Locksmith blinked. "No. But she knew she was close to figuring it out. Over the next day she hacked off more and more of her own body. I feared the process would kill her. I think it would have, if she hadn't cycled through her attempts in such a fierce frenzy that no infection had time to take hold."

"She got it right in the end?"

Locksmith nodded his chin at Stranger's bloody shoulder socket. "Humerus. After she cut her arm off, she told me I had to help her. Together we made the key, and I had to carry her to the door, she was so injured by that point. It worked, and she was gone."

Locksmith did not meet Stranger's eyes. There wasn't a day—no, a second—when he didn't regret helping her make that key.

"And then you made a business out of it."

Stranger said it without judgment, but Locksmith's stomach twisted anyway. "I didn't intend to, but people began to come to me, having heard about my sister. They wanted to know how she had done it, and whether I could help them too. I shouldn't have charged, but things got tough and, well, I have to eat."

He searched Stranger's face for the forgiveness he craved.

Stranger nodded. "The sand is killing everyone. I'm sorry about your sister."

Locksmith smiled, and waited, shifting the majority of his weight onto his good foot. Stranger's eyes flickered closed again.

"That's the end of my story," he said, just in case it wasn't clear. If Stranger wanted to share his story, Locksmith wanted him to know he could. But Stranger didn't reply. A snore tore from his nose, even though he was still sitting upright.

"Sweet dreams," Locksmith whispered, and backed out of the room.

***

The sky outside shrank into the earth, growing a dense orange. Locksmith's workbench faced out the window, and sunset was his favorite time to work. One day, he believed, the sky would grow so heavy it would fall around the little globe and suffocate it. His mother's favorite story for sunsets, the three of them huddled on the sill. Locksmith longed for the kinds of stories his mother might invent about the desert, had she lived to see it. She'd reveled in fear, often saying it was the very reason she was alive.

Whittling delicate, brittle bone was far different to iron. Locksmith often wondered how these porous structures could support a human. It made him feel weak. He used simple tools: chisel, knife, flame. The key blackened where he burned it, and summoned a stench akin to that of singed hair. Still, there was a sickly, tingling excitement to crafting a bone key. Stranger was present while Locksmith worked, even if he himself did not know it. Locksmith needed a story to focus his mind on, to help his hands while they worked. He used the feeling he got from their interactions, brief as they may have been. But he wanted more, ached for Stranger's story. And so he invented a story for this man in his house. A tale of a lost man who'd lost his sister, and wanted to meet up with her so badly he had sacrificed his arm, and was willing to risk sacrificing much more. Were those who went through the door the pessimists or the optimists?

At the end, he scraped delicately, fine-tuning. The fledgling key hummed as he shaped it. Secrets divulged in a foreign language, told but not heard. When he was finished, Locksmith placed the unused portion of the humerus with the others, in a wooden box with seals to fight the sand. He kept them all together, hoping they might give one another comfort. He packed the morose, broken pieces with expensive velvet and Himalayan salt. The box contained bones from all over the human skeleton. It was curious to him which bones different people chose to sacrifice. Some wished to retain their ability to walk, while others viewed their arms as indispensable. More rare in his collection were a hip bone, and from one particularly bright-eyed teenage girl he kept the tiny remains of her ear bones, an ear she had sliced off and dissected herself. Locksmith remembered her fondly. He'd been unsure whether he could combine little bones to make a larger key, but she had insisted he try, and it had worked. Her final key contained some of the smallest, most delicate bones in the human body. Malleus. Incus. Stapes.

It was important to remember them. He rested the remains of Stranger's humerus among the others, in the almost-center position. Every new bone took the almost-center, his love for the recent always strongest, with one exception. At the center of the box, his sister's vast collection of discarded bones cradled together in their velvet wrappings. Locksmith brought her humerus to his lips and kissed it. Were those on the other side of the bone door safe?

***

A new cup of tea for his guest steamed in Locksmith's hand, this one containing a sprinkle of nutmeg. Stranger stirred at the sound of the door, but it was clear he'd managed to rest, and Locksmith's heart swelled at how peaceful he looked, how warm, and how his eyebrows twitched in bleary confusion. Locksmith hated how easily he loved each of his bone clients, a fleeting kind of adoration which fought the sand away for as long as it lasted, for as long as it took him to make their key and aid them through the door, and then for a little while after. The key in his other hand thrummed. Locksmith closed his fist around it and let the beat soak through his blood. He always felt melancholy on these mornings. It chased away the blasted, ever-present hunger. He would walk to the village that afternoon and buy some food with Stranger's coins and distract himself from the goodbye. Stranger looked up and his eyes were a little brighter.

"Did you make it?"

Locksmith unwrapped his fingers. The key was a little shorter than the span of his hand, skinny and intricate, with blackened edges along the cuts. Beyond the shoulder, the bow swept round into an oval, with an asymmetric star cut out its middle. Stranger set his teacup on the sand-strewn floor to accept the key. He looked as if he might be sick as he traced with his finger the shape of the grooves. Then, he slowly curled his hand around it, one finger at a time.

"I want to go now."

Locksmith panicked. "But you haven't finished your tea," he said, more forcefully than his guest deserved.

Stranger laughed, the first time Locksmith had ever heard the sound. It surprised him pleasantly, a soft and gentle chuckle, splashed with a hint of pity.

"If I wait, I may never go."

Locksmith understood.

***

The door was close, just over a dune. Stranger walked a little ahead even though it was Locksmith who knew the way. Stranger's body seemed to thrum, fuelled with anxiety or excitement, while Locksmith's own body ached as he limped up the dune. But when he caught sight of the door he sped up, his gait uncontrollable. The door presented itself at least twice the width and triple the height of any grand, man-made door. It looked lonely and incomplete, a door in a frame, standing without walls in the middle of a desert. It was made of brass, with a peacock frame which seemed to bleed into the metal, little blue grooves swirling into intricate patterns, the color draining moments before they reached the center. The lock that had drawn so much attention was a plain, humble thing compared to the rest of the door.

Stranger encircled the door twice, his mouth hanging open and wondering, Locksmith was sure, as he had often wondered himself, how such a door could lead somewhere else entirely, and not the patch of sand behind it. Locksmith did not follow him. He had circled it hundreds of times. Thousands. Instead, he pressed a hand against it, splaying his fingers, letting his pulse map the tiny grooves, which were always ice-cool in contrast to the sunlit brass. The door always emitted a sound—a sweet susurration, like the hiss of cool water through a pipe. His other palm joined, then Locksmith pressed his forehead against the brass too, in silent prayer until Stranger joined his side once more and he straightened.

"The sand hasn't eroded it," Stranger observed.

"I polish it myself." Locksmith's chest swelled at Stranger's noticing. Even if nobody else thought it important to maintain, it was. He dusted the sand from his arms again, but even this subtle breeze, too weak to ripple his clothing, returned it to his skin. Stranger copied, but watched Locksmith as he did so. He looked deep in thought.

"Do you ever wish you had a key of your own?" he asked. Locksmith met his eyes, his heart fluttering. He had never shown anyone before. But Stranger was different, he told himself, even though he knew it likely wasn't true, even though they all seemed different at the time. His hand dived into the depths of his pocket before he could stop himself, and pulled out a black velvet cloth. He shook it free of sand and uncovered the key that he polished every day while he drank tea on his windowsill. He'd carved it from a bone he'd sliced off his foot, the day after his sister left. Hallux. A shocked smile curled Stranger's lips.

"Then why do you hesitate?"

Locksmith trickled his fingers down the icy grooves. The door's humming thrummed deep within his veins. He wrapped and pocketed the key. If he ever left, who would craft bone keys for people like Stranger?

"If you're so curious," Stranger pressed, "why don't you come?"

Stranger did not hold out his hand, but Locksmith imagined that he did, and his own palm sweated its eagerness to curl around Stranger's fingers.

"Come back to the workshop and I'll tell you." The words shot out of him at rapid speed, and he looked down guiltily at the rippling sand.

"What?"

"Just...consider it a little longer. You have your key ready. I'll give you a refund if you don't use it." His heart raced, heat waves rippling before his eyes. He couldn't think properly, he just wanted Stranger to stay.

"Refund?" Stranger's brow creased. "You don't know how many years of sleepless nights I've spent deliberating this. I'm going today. Besides, you need the money, my friend."

Friend. Locksmith curled a hand around Stranger's wounded shoulder. He meant it to be reassuring, but Stranger flinched backwards.

"It's a mistake." Locksmith croaked out a grain of sand which had been lodged in his throat, and found himself hurling a mismatch of arguments at Stranger. His mouth mixed together truths and lies which his tongue twisted sourly around. "The sandstorms only sweep in one direction—towards the door. Call it geography, prevailing winds influenced by a complex network of factors—the moon and tides and the battles that occur when hot air smashes into cold air high above our heads. I don't care. It isn't the truth of this sand. It arrived with the door, and I believe it will stay as long as there are people on this side. It ushers us all towards it. Perhaps with noble intentions, but the sand is not renowned for its helpfulness, is it? Listen, I've seen the faces on those that leave. I've seen regret when they open the door. Don't let that be you," he panted, his mind jumping from thought to thought, trying to cohere more panicked words to offer Stranger.

Stanger stared at Locksmith, and the door held its breath. It was wrong, Locksmith knew. The decision belonged to them, like the key. If they were the last things that would ever belong to them, they ought to be truly, undeniably, theirs. But how many people could Locksmith bear to lose?

"I have to go," Stranger said, somehow firmer this time. "Thank you for my key." There was a chill to his words, as if he had already vanished from the desert. He turned away.

Locksmith nodded, and left. It was all he could do, now the damage was done. Locksmith didn't want to watch Stranger leave. He wanted to return home, drink tea on his windowsill, polish all the bones, and wait for a new customer so he might forget about Stranger. He did not say goodbye, for he hoped that it was not. Besides, his voice would betray his emotions. He gave Stranger a small nod and wave, then climbed the dune, his foot aching but the rest of his body persevering. Quickly was the only way to travel these days. Quickly, or the sand burned you, perhaps lashing out in anger after years of being burned itself by the sun. He dizzied in the heat, as if everything in the world swiveled in those moments and left Locksmith where he was, a tiny observer in a great desert.

But at the top of the dune, Locksmith stopped and turned. Stranger had not yet passed through the door—instead, he was watching Locksmith. When he saw Locksmith look, he darted his gaze back to the door, as if suddenly remembering why he was there, missing an arm, holding what was probably the most expensive item he'd ever bought. He slotted the key into the door, and Locksmith imagined the satisfying click of bone against bone. With his back to Locksmith, Stranger's expression was hidden when he opened the door. Locksmith imagined he smiled. He hoped he smiled. Then, a second later, he stepped through.

Did Stranger and the others remember Locksmith on the other side of the bone door?

The Price of Pearls

E. Fox

E. Fox is a mother, lawyer, and writer. She braids her late-blooming queerness, Texan sensibilities, and faith into her poetry and prose. Some of her poems can be found at Brazos River Review, Cordella Magazine, and Susurrus Literary Magazine.

Only fearful men burn silver runes into their boats' bones.

I know that, now, but I did not know that the first time that I saw Ivor's longboat plowing rough and proud through the bright foam.

He smelled of otter bones and cold iron. I thought him harmless—just another Yupredok fisherman—nothing to fear from him, he wasn't a wild woman come to smash my heart. He wasn't Valfa, orca-cruel and beautiful, he did not scare me.

I felt certain then that the worst possible future was a loveless one.

I will never again be so stupid.

Ivor laughed as he sailed past, and waved gaily to the rookery; he probably thought I was simply another seal lured to Rovani Bay by sweet fish and fat puffins.

He probably thought that I, too, was harmless.

I think perhaps Ivor will never again be so stupid, either.

***

Every morning the Yupredok fisherfolk would set sail, cupping clay mugs of cinnamon tea, and they would return when their nets were full. Some of the boats split the salt spray with dragon-carved prows; other boats boasted intricate sculptures of griffins or striped unicorns.

Only Ivor's boat shimmered with metal wards.

Sunglazed and glutted on eels, I did not immediately notice her, the first time she came down from the village to the glittering beach. But the puffins puttering across the sand did, and they all took to the sky at once in a cloudburst of feathers.

I opened just one eye, I remember, because the day was all pink and gold, and sleep's song hummed warm through my blood.

But then I saw her, and I bolted awake. Beside me, another seal grumbled and splashed irate into the water.

I did not care.

She was short, muscle laced, with dark curls that frothed unruly over broad shoulders. Her dress was wool, a shade slipped between blue and green, and cinched about her waist. Freckles dappled her nose and cheeks and the skin of her forearms. She was not sleek, like Valfa, not slender nor luminous nor beautiful.

Yet there was something about her, some ineffable iridescence that flashed and then melted away, the way a pearl shimmers just before the oyster snaps shut.

I watched as she walked across the black sand, parallel to the waves, revealing a man behind her. Bundled in slick otter pelts, he stood square to the sea, watching the horizon.

"I told you that there is nothing here to see."

"Yes, there is! Look at the seals, how fearsome they are when they yawn. And these birds!" She pointed at the puffins, who had settled on a high cliff overlooking the beach.

"Ah, yes, puffins, ridiculous birds. They're so stupid that they are afraid of you, Kastsha!" The man I now know as Ivor chuckled at his own joke.

"Why shouldn't they be afraid? They know I am your wife, the mother of your children, and you will protect me from whatever mischief they're plotting."

I watched her smile, and her teeth flashed, and for a hot moment I imagined they were sharp and set against my throat.

"Yes, the puffins would do well to remember that. Do you hear? She is mine!" Ivor bellowed playfully, shaking his fist at the sun.

He did not face the sanctuary crags where the puffins perched, though. He faced the seal rookery.

He faced me.

***

Kastsha visited the shore a few times after that; Ivor always accompanied her. And every time she stepped onto the beach, the puffins fled and Ivor laughed. Eventually she came with baskets of dried bread; I could see in the set of her jawbone that she was determined to convince the birds to stay, one way or another.

She was stubborn, and that made her beautiful.

On good days, the wind would shift and I would catch her scent: salt and leather and a thread of cold, powdery redolence that I could not identify.

Kastsha was tempting, yes, but even still, I did not consider her worth the considerable risk. Not after Valfa.

So I was content simply to watch her, the way one might admire the lancing glory of faraway lightning.

But Ivor made a fool's mistake, coming down to the ocean so often wrapped in his otter furs. Puffins are malicious gossipmongers, and Ivor had called them stupid.

Soon the sea otters arrived.

***

Humans fear sharks and whales and everything larger than themselves, I think. *Tyulki* fear very little, for we have a bit of our own magic as well as our unnatural strength. Yet I keep a respectful distance from sea otters, if I can. They weave deft and powerful enchantments using kelp and coral; their weakest spells are stronger than anything we *tyulki* might do, because otters never cast alone, and for that, I envied them.

So when Hefna and Forset came ashore in the night, star-spangled with saltwater, and asked for the shifting leopard seal of Rovani Bay, I answered.

Otters smash clams against jagged rocks so that they can dine on their innards. They treat their enemies no differently.

From the puffins they had learned of Ivor and his thick otter coat; from the dolphins they had learned of his silver-warded boat. I told them that I knew nothing else about the man, except that he had children and a wife.

Hefna tilted her head and fixed me with a black glare.

"We know of his wife. We know more about her than you, Svashosha."

"I am sure you do."

I did not ask how they knew my name. That did not matter to me. But, oh, how I wanted to fall upon Hefna and devour her. She knew more about Kastsha than I, and there is no hunger more savage than sudden jealousy.

"Have you ever wondered why there was no other *tyulki* here when you arrived? The bay is rich with prey, isn't it?" Forset, serene and calm, stacked smooth stones as he spoke. The pile curved like a spine, unsteady and pale in the moonlight.

"That man did not work silver into his boat to protect himself from us," Hefna bared her milky fangs. "Humans do not know what otters are, we make certain of that."

"He is afraid of something else. Can you guess, shifter?" The clack of Forset's pebbles matched his tone's implacable rhythm. "Do you see, yet?"

I snarled, then, because I do not like games and I like feeling foolish even less than that.

"Do not play with me, or treat me like some idiot pup. I am not as powerful as you, but I am older," I snapped my jaws shut over Forset's head. "And my teeth are longer."

Hefna laughed, unafraid, and looped the length of her body around her mate.

"Save your anger, Svashosha. Save it for Ivor, who found his wife ashore on this beach after a full moon and convinced her that she was utterly unremarkable. And utterly human."

"Is she not...?"

And then I understood why I could see Kastsha's freckles when I closed my eyes; why they seemed so familiar to me, even as they spread across her pale and hairless skin.

"But...how?"

"Silver, we think. You know she cannot change back, not even in salt water, if she is silver bound. She would know too, or should know, but she does not. Whatever storm spat her ashore must have battered her mind, wiped it as clean as the beach after high tide." Forset swept his tail across the sand, erasing the lingering curves left by lapping waves.

"And what...why did you come here? Why did you tell me?"

"Because Ivor hunts our animal kin. You saw his coat." Hefna's bottomless eyes flashed. "Because it is a betrayal of the ancient ways to trap a magical thing in a cage. Even if that cage looks like a home or a family."

"And because we cannot help her," Forset added. "We cannot go so far into a human village without drawing unwanted attention. But the full moon is tomorrow, isn't it?"

"So I will go." It was not a question. I did not hesitate. "You want me to free her."

"Yes. And you will bring Ivor to the beach." Hefna flicked her paw against the topmost stone, and the tower clattered down. "For us."

***

Every *tyulki* feels differently about the skin shift. There are those who detest it, those who choose never to walk ashore on human legs— and there are some of us who enjoy, perhaps perversely, the crackle of bone, and the way our muscles pool around our newly moon-sculpted shapes.

In the breath between sunset and moonrise, I met Hefna and Forset in the shallows. Together they held a crown of plaited land flowers adorned with luminous chips of abalone shell.

"For me?" The flowers' perfume was sweet but also dry, and hot, the way earth smells after a blazing summer day.

They smelled just like Kastsha.

"No." Hefna lifted one purple petal and sniffed. "Violets, humans call these."

"We worked through the night and dawn to braid this." Forset thumped his tail into the wet sand. "It will call Kastsha back to herself."

"But do not place it on her head if she still wears silver, any silver at all, or it will not work," Hefna cautioned.

I glanced to the horizon—a white sliver of the early moon shimmered in both sea and sky. I nodded. Immediately they understood, and stepped back so that I might let the magic work its way through my blood.

Swiftly the change happened, as it always does. Yet for me, this time, it felt as an eternity, and I did not know why. Perhaps my heart could not tolerate any delay because of Kastsha, locked in chains she could not recognize.

I knew my human form well. I had not yet walked among the Yupredok, but I was old, and I had visited many other women in many other villages. Hefna and Forset placed the crown into my waiting palms.

"We hid things for you, just past the beach, in the crook of an elder willow. He was very happy to help," Hefna grinned, and I shivered in spite of myself, though not from cold.

"A dress, some boots, and a knife." Forset was already wading further into the waves. "A small knife, *tyulki*."

"You do not want me to hurt him." I nodded and started to wade toward land. Toward her.

"Oh, no, Svashosha, you are welcome to hurt him," Hefna chirped, before she disappeared beneath the dark water. "But we will kill him."

***

I found the clothing and knife exactly where Hefna said they would be, safely tucked between the gnarled roots of a beach willow scarred by a thousand storms. Sea glass chimes glimmered among vibrant leaves; Yupredok fishermen must have placed them there, maybe to sound as a musical boundary between shore and village.

Remembering Hefna's words, I dipped my head respectfully as I yanked the kelp-wrapped packet free of its hiding place.

"I am no sea otter, Tree, but if you might protect me while I dress myself, I would appreciate it."

For a moment I thought myself absurd, drunk still on the skin shift, but then I heard the creak of wood and the salt breeze whisper of leaves.

Willow branches surrounded me.

I swallowed. It was one thing to hear about sea otter magic and another thing entirely to see it. Quickly I slid into the gown and tucked the knife into my belt; around my left shoulder I coiled the enchanted violet crown.

"Thank you." I bowed this time, before starting on the cobblestone path to the Yupredok village.

Everything was uniform and gray— gray stone homes and shops, with thick, weather-bleached thatching. Only the doors offered a bit of color: spirals of red paint lacquered atop pale pine.

I thought perhaps that Hefna had blessed my gown with good fortune, because it was laughably easy to track Ivor. He was the only man brazen enough to hunt otters and wear their pelts, and their oily pungence could never be scrubbed away nor hidden. I silently thanked him for his arrogance as I rounded a bend in the cobbled road.

"May I help you, madam?"

Fiercely focused on Ivor's stench, I did not notice the wizened man walking behind me until he spoke. I turned, slowly, calmly, and licked my suddenly dry lips, for I had not spoken a human tongue in many years.

"Ah, yes, I am here to visit my friend, Kastsha...do you know where she lives?"

He considered me with clear eyes. Around his neck twined a golden torque, orca-engraved and set with blue gemstones.

"I think you know exactly where she lives, as you have made a raven's straight path to her home."

Beneath his braided beard, his mouth drifted up into a wry smile. "And she does not have many friends here, our Kastsha. Ivor is very...protective."

"I have heard." I relaxed, just a little.

"Have you now?" He glanced up to the night sky, and chuckled. "Well, word does have a way of getting around when puffins are involved."

Shock darted across my face before I could catch myself.

"Be warned, madam." With a flourish of his homespun robes, he gestured toward Ivor's scarlet door. "He will not let you in, not under any pretense, because he has been expecting one of you ever since he stole sweet Kastsha from the shore."

"Then I will have to hope she comes out of her house..."

"She will if it suits him, and I imagine your otter luck has yet to run out."

Again, I started and again he laughed.

"Thank you for your help..."

"Mazek. Elder Mazek. There are those of us here in Rovani who respect the ocean and all that She hides. I only ask that you remember that."

"Elder, why didn't you help her, if you know what she is?" I did not bother to bite back the question that bubbled sharp and quick from my mouth.

"Well." He twisted one of his braids about his forefinger. "It was none of my business, I suppose."

And then Mazek carried on down the cobbled road, humming to himself, as though he had not just met a *tyulki* under the full moon.

None of his business? I inhaled deeply, once, twice, thrice, to quell my rising fury. Killing Mazek wouldn't free Kastsha, I reminded myself.

I padded silently into the fragrant cypress shrubs flanking Ivor's home. I realized he must be a hunter of great wealth and standing, to have this much glass set into his windows—to feel as though the ocean owed him all of its most precious prizes.

The knife was in my hand before I realized my fingers had moved.

"The children are asleep, my love."

"Ah, very good, Kastsha." Ivor's voice boomed more clearly through the walls, and he lumbered past the window. I could smell that damn coat. "I want some eggs, fried in butter, and a glass of akavit."

Not a trace of courtesy softened his tone. He spoke as a man who expected things simply to happen as he wished.

"Of course." Kastsha's voice, plush and pliant, made my heart ache. "Why don't you take off your boots, darling, and I'll be right back."

A wooden creak splintered the quiet. Kastsha opened the front door and slipped out, picking her way through the yard toward the low chicken coop. I could have reached out then to grab her wrist, I could have dragged her screaming all the way to the beach and beyond, but I was frozen, transfixed by the liquid way she moved and the way the moonlight seemed to leap from freckle to freckle under her eyes, shimmering but never settling.

She paused in the thick of a sprawling herb garden and tilted her head back to the starry sky. At her throat silver glinted: a thick chain dripping with tiny pearls arrayed to look like rain.

Or tears.

"Kastsha," I whispered, first, then more loudly: "Kastsha."

She turned to face me, her curls foamed around her face, her mouth half-open in surprise.

"Who are you?"

"A friend," I jammed the knife back into my belt and held out empty palms.

"Well, stranger, I have no use for friends," Kastsha replied. "I have all I could ever need here, with my family, and if you are here to hurt me, know that my husband is the strongest man in the entire village."

Even still, Kastsha did not scream for him, though we both knew Ivor would hear and come running at once. It seemed she wanted something but she did not know how to name it.

"I would never dream of hurting you." She could not know how truly I spoke. "That is a pretty chain. Did your husband give it to you?" I sidled closer. Her eyes flicked toward the house, then down to her silver and pearls.

"He did."

"Was it a gift? Or an exchange?"

"An...exchange?" Kastsha's brows splashed together.

"Did you give something up for this...trinket?" I purposefully barbed my question with derision.

"No."

"Are you so certain?" As I pressed, I saw the first sharp flash of anger in the depths of her eyes. My beautiful thunderstorm.

"Yes!"

"Then may I look at it? Your necklace? I know pearls very well, you see. I have always loved them, because they remind me of the sea even when I cannot be there."

"Are you going to steal it?" Sweet, guileless Kastsha. I would rather die than touch silver, but the momentary pain would be worth it.

"No, not at all. I merely want to check the craftsmanship, to make sure it is as valuable as you deserve. I will give you my crown to hold as surety."

From around my shoulder I unslung the violet and abalone garland, and I held it out in the thin space between us. She hesitated, just for a moment, and then pulled the chain up and over her head.

"I love the sea, too, but I rarely get a moment to go down to the shore." Kastsha traced a flower petal with a single, gentle finger while I pretended to examine her necklace. In truth, it took all of my willpower not to hiss and drop the cursed thing in the soil. Ivor must have clasped the chain around her neck while she was still storm-stunned, or else she would have felt its harsh and burning chill.

"Kastsha, these pearls are very valuable, and indeed, beautiful." I inhaled slowly and let my exhalation carry a wave of pain out into the night air. "As are you."

"I..." Her fingers flew to the hollow of her throat, now empty. "Thank you."

"Svashosha. My name is Svashosha." The pain was impossible to ignore now, but I knew like the tide it would ebb away, so I focused on Kastsha's heart-shaped face, and the freckled constellations on her cheekbones. "Before I return your necklace, you should try on my crown. It suits you."

"Do you think?"

"I do, yes, very much."

She lifted the garland to her head and I held my breath.

"Kastsha? What is taking so long?" Ivor's face blocked the wash of light pooling beneath the glass pane window. I could see the way his forehead creased, the way the muscles tightened against his jaw, and then he slammed his hand violently against the window.

Ivor knew what I was. He knew why I was here, in his herb garden, with his magnificent wife. Light blazed again from the casement as he dashed away, toward the front door.

I hoped Kastsha would forgive me. I lunged forward and wrapped my arms around her.

"I am sorry," I whispered against the shell of her ear, and then I yanked the flowers around her head. As they slipped over her hair to her forehead, the violets seemed to absorb the moonglow, blazing even more brilliant than the dawn sky.

When something dies in the ocean, it dies silently. I had never heard a scream like Kastsha's before, nor do I ever want to hear anything like it ever again. Keening, she might have fallen to her knees, tears cascading from her suddenly haunted eyes, but I seized both of her wrists and jerked her after me as I bolted toward the seaward path.

Ivor exploded, howling, through the front door.

I did not look back. I knew he was there; he still had on his fur coat, and I could smell that, mixed with the sour sweat of an angry huntsman.

Kastsha knew he was behind us, as well. I wasted no breath speaking, because I did not have to; I merely looked at her, and she answered me with a decisive nod, though her tears had not stopped. We sprinted past Elder Willow and onto the shore, and I laughed in spite of myself, because the tide was high and we were so close to freedom.

But then Kastsha collapsed, sobbing, and the sound of Ivor's boots shifted from heavy thudding to rasping stride as he hurtled from the stone path to sand.

"No, no, Kastsha, you know we have to get into the water, and we must go now..."

"You will take her nowhere." Ivor loomed large in the night, and he pointed at me with an unshaking finger. In his other hand he held a jagged spear with the limber ease of someone who knew how to skewer prey through shifting water. "I knew one of you might come, one day, but she is mine!"

"She is not." I positioned myself between them, and I snarled, though born from a human throat, it emerged as a weak and pitiful growl.

"She is. I found her. She belongs to me."

"I am not yours." Kastsha's breath was ragged, waterlogged, but I could hear the *tyulki* strength returning to her, so I started to move backwards, slowly, toward the waves.

"Was I so bad to you, Kastsha? Did I ever hurt you, the way some of the men do? I never once slapped you, never once did I throw you against the wall, or threaten you with the fire irons," Ivor wheedled.

"I wish you had." Kastsha stood, and she glared at Ivor with a strange, furious tenderness. "I wish you had beaten me until bruises outnumbered my freckles. That would have been better than hiding me from myself."

I reached out to take Kastsha's hand, and I clasped her palm with my own chain-wrapped fingers. She could feel the bite of the silver, now, but still she lifted her chin defiantly.

"You would forswear your children?" Ivor stepped forward and spread his arms. "You would abandon them?"

Kastsha flinched, then, and in that moment I hated Ivor more than I had ever hated anything.

"Was it real, Svashosha? What I felt for my babes...my pups... was it real?"

I rested my cheek on her shoulder, hoping she might draw strength from the press of my ribs against hers, and I whispered, "Yes, it was real. It is real, even now. He made you forget yourself, but it was your heart that made you a mother."

Kastsha gripped my belt as though to steady herself, and I felt her sigh. Ivor moved forward again; I tried to pull Kastsha back toward the water with me, but she was frozen in place.

"I knew you would see reason, my love." Ivor stabbed the spear into the ground and reached out to take her back into his arms, heedless of the slick kelp knot beneath his boots.

Never cross sea otters: Ivor's last lesson.

A trill rang out through the night, and then a deeper chirp laced through the lilting melody, and the kelp stretched impossibly, twisting up and twining tightly around Ivor's burly frame and across his mouth.

He tried to fight, of course, but then he could not be expected to know any better.

Hefna slithered from the shallows first, and Forset followed.

"Svashosha." She tipped her head to me, and the diamond droplets on her whiskers shivered and fell. Then she turned to Kastsha.

"I grieve for your loss."

Kastsha smiled, a sick and wounded smile, and nodded.

"Thank you for sending Svashosha."

"I think she would have come for you without our help," Forset sniffed. "In time."

"Yes." I blushed for the first time, and I squeezed Kastsha's hand again.

"I am sorry," she whispered, and all at once I felt the missing heft of the knife, and she was lunging for Ivor.

More quickly than I could see, more magical kelp tangled about her ankles, and Kastsha tumbled with a dull thud.

"We want him to suffer, Kastsha. Do you see his coat? Those otters were our family." Hefna did not sound angry, which surprised me.

"I want him to suffer, too," Kastsha murmured, and she pushed herself up to her arms and knees. Yet when she looked up, she was crying again. "But I cannot let my children be alone, without anyone, in that house with its red door."

And the knife tumbled from her nerveless grip.

Hefna nodded, and Forset began to dig something up from beneath the sand.

"We had kits, very long ago. They are grown now." Forset straightened. Between his paws he held a small driftwood poppet, roughly carved to look like a human wearing an overlarge coat.

"We know what it means to love your children. We know that you might give up everything— vengeance, freedom, your soul— for them. And we do not want that." Hefna's whiskers quivered almost imperceptibly. "So, please pick up the knife, Kastsha, and do as we ask."

Kastsha's seaweed binding melted into nothingness. She bent, stiffly, and palmed the little blade Forset had given me.

"Give me your violet crown, and then cut a hank of his hair." Forset accepted the flower wreath from Kastsha, and as he took the crown, it stopped glowing. I watched him yank a few stems from the garland, and he began to plait them into a tighter weave. Silently, so that Kastsha could not see, I slipped him her pearls and silver chain.

I should not have worried that she might have noticed. Kastsha was focused entirely on Ivor, who continued to thrash against his slick shackles. She crouched next to him, and pressed the tip of the blade into his chin, so that he was forced to behold her.

"You will love my children as I did. As I do. You will bring them to the shore, every full moon, so that I might see them, and touch them. And if they..." Kastsha swallowed a swelling sob. "If they are as I am, I will take them, and you will never see them again."

Over his seaweed gag, Ivor's eyes widened in disbelief. For a moment I thought Kastsha might still slit his throat. He would have deserved that, and more, but she merely sliced a handful of his hunter's braids.

"You will do as she says, Ivor, Sea-Hated." Forset took the braids into his deft paws and tucked them into the poppet's new violet and silver bindings. Kastsha stumbled back to me, and I held her as tightly as I could.

Hefna pulled a glittering sea urchin spine from seemingly nowhere; perhaps a dark wind brought it to her. Without warning, she shoved it into the poppet's right arm.

Ivor's scream was not so heartbreaking as Kastsha's had been.

"You will do as she says, will you not?"

Ivor nodded, and nodded, and kept nodding.

Hefna and Forset turned away from him, and they bowed, once to me, and once to Kastsha.

"We will build a new holt, here, in Rovani Bay, *tyulki*. We will stay, and we promise to make sure he upholds his promises to you."

"Thank you," Kastsha freed a shuddering breath.

I pointed to where the moon had dipped almost entirely behind the water's edge. "I think it is time we go."

And so, hand in hand, we did.

***

Though many high tides have come and gone, Kastsha still visits her children. They are nearly grown, now, and they are both shape changers like their mother, though they are not *tyulki*. Blending our blood with that of the earthbound humans resulted in some altogether different magic. The Yupredok honor them, though, so Kastsha does not fear for them, and she taught them about the dangers of silver, and the treachery of losing yourself.

Kastsha has healed as much as she ever will, but I know deep in her heart, where even I cannot reach, a hurricane brews.

Sometimes, she will find a rocky island not far from land, and she will slide back into her human skin, all wild hair and wild eyes and wild song.

Fishermen who try to catch her always drown.

Crowd Demons

Lisa Farrell

Lisa Farrell lives and writes in the UK. Her stories have been published by Mslexia and the British Fantasy Society, and performed by Liars' League London.

I first came across the phenomenon when commissioned to photograph guests at a grand soiree. With so many ladies and gentlemen in high spirits, it was impossible to compel them to behave; they simply would not remain still long enough to achieve a satisfactory tableau. I therefore gathered them in smaller groups: four or five posing for a picture while the masses remained unfocussed behind them. This would satisfy my client, I hoped, though he'd seemed the difficult type—a gentleman whose nose could easily be put out of joint. I took a dozen pictures or so, and left.

However, when I came to develop the photographs, there were few that I would dare put my name to. Many were spoiled by a strange phenomenon, a coalition of shadows manifesting as frightful faces in the spaces between or behind my subjects. Had such appeared only in one image, I might have thought it the result of my weary gaze and the random fabric of the crowd. Yet I found these blurred faces in so many of the pictures that I could not dismiss their presence so easily.

Now, I am familiar with so-called 'spirit photography', but I have never subscribed to the notion that ghosts might be caught on camera. Besides, these faces were not human enough to be considered visages of the departed. The faces were indistinct, yet enough of their features were clear that there could be no mistaking their nature. Teeth like daggers and horns curling to a point, along with malicious expressions at odds with the pursed lips and smooth brows of the guests...These were not the faces of people in the crowd, caught fleetingly. These were visions of demons.

I took the few photographs I deemed acceptable to my client the next day, prepared to apologise that there were not more. On reaching the drive of his grand house however, I found a police-search underway. My presence being instantly detected, they enquired as to my business, and I was questioned thoroughly about the events of the night before. They would not tell me precisely what had occurred, but it was clear that some serious crime had taken place. Moreover, they informed me that my client could not receive me and seized my photographs for their investigation. I did not mention those pictures I had locked safely away.

It was only when an article appeared in *The Times* that I learned what had happened. On that evening several otherwise respectable ladies and gentlemen had attacked one another in a sort of mania, scratching with nails and teeth. Many were injured, and several afterwards sent to an asylum for treatment. My client himself had lost the tip of his nose in the fracas. Recalling the gay atmosphere of the evening I found this all difficult to imagine, and yet I thought of those unexplained, demonic faces in the pictures, and I wondered if there was something to them.

I have never been superstitious, preferring to look to science rather than folklore to make sense of the modern world. Nevertheless, I kept a close eye on the papers and came across several cases of 'crowd mayhem', as the journalists called it. Groups of otherwise civilised people enjoying themselves in the city of an evening, inexplicably turning to bestial violence. Friends, relations, it didn't seem to matter; if the group was large, or company condensed, mayhem could occur. The police were puzzled; after all, this new phenomenon appeared to be inexplicable.

I couldn't go to the police with some insubstantial theory and a few blurry photographs, so I undertook my own experiment. The sites afflicted so far were popular haunts, places I knew to be usually pleasant to visit, but they were closed for investigation. So, each evening I gathered my equipment and sought crowds: shoppers in the streets, audiences at concerts, busy dockyards, and a variety of drinking establishments. I took pictures of crowds of all kinds across the city.

Developing those photographs, my hands trembled. I did not want to find more of those demonic faces, and yet a part of me wanted to be right. Perhaps it was my vanity, simply the wish to be correct in my deductions, or maybe I was hoping an external agent was the cause of the mayhem that otherwise must be attributed to some failing of human nature. Blame demons and those people who tore at each other's flesh become innocent victims.

The faces appeared again, this time in every single photograph I'd taken. In fact, there were more faces than I'd revealed at that fateful soiree. Some I recognised from picture to picture, and one in particular stood out: a long face with a pointed chin and protruding snakelike tongue, with eyes that looked directly at the camera. In one image, that face superseded all others, so close to the lens I could detect something like intelligence in those eyes.

I'd been taking photographs for years, portraits of the living and dead, and I'd never come across anything like this before. I didn't want to risk my reputation, but I felt the public had a right to know. Still, I hesitated. I continued to examine the papers and sure enough, over the next few days, incidents were reported at all the venues I'd visited. Crowd mayhem had spread like a disease across the city. Women were warned to ensure they were home by twilight. The police remained baffled.

I could have taken the photographs to the police, or perhaps a man of the church, but I wasn't yet sure enough in my convictions. People might believe I had engineered the images somehow, or worse, think I had a hand in the events since my presence had preceded so many. Yet I had to speak to someone. I decided to visit somewhere I could expect to be seriously considered: The Society of Demonological Research.

I took a cab to the headquarters of the society, a nondescript terraced building with a curious symbol marked above the door. It was the shape of an eye, divided by a jagged line. Examining it made my own eyes water, so I turned my attention to the door and knocked. Clutching my pictures to my chest, I requested admittance, and was announced to a small company.

Three elderly men sat around a table in a cramped sitting-room, warmed beyond reason by a smoky fire in the grate behind them. They did not greet me or ask my business, but blinked at me as though I had come to be studied. I sweated under their gaze for a moment and decided to get straight to the point.

"Gentlemen, I have come to ask your advice," I said, and placed my pictures on the table one by one. The gentlemen immediately turned their full attention to the evidence before them. Yet, they did not seem startled by the images, and their questions when they came were of an unexpected sort.

"Have you ever seen the demons when alone?" they enquired. "Or heard them? Or talked to them?"

They seemed more concerned about my personal experiences than the phenomenon itself.

"Are you suggesting these faces have something to do with me?" I asked. "I've taken many pictures before, and there have been no such faces. They only appear in crowds. Then, terrible things happen. You must have seen the papers. People turn on each other. It's horrendous. We must do something."

The three men looked at each other.

"There is something we can do," said one, "but there is no need to traipse about the city chasing demons if we locate the source."

I took offence at the implication in their accusing looks and would have left, only one calmly offered to buy my pictures for a handsome sum and asked to commission a photograph. I was glad to be recompensed for my labours, and I never turn down a commission. I offered to return with my equipment the next day, but they insisted on coming instead to meet me at my workshop. To this I agreed.

I spent a fitful night, thinking over their questions. The more I told myself that it was only crowds I need fear, the more the floors of my apartment seemed to creak, and the windows rattle. I even, as I closed my eyes, fancied I heard breathing at my ear.

Next morning I rose wearily and prepared my equipment. I tried to light the fire but it would not catch, and the room was unnaturally cold. My sitters arrived with equipment of their own, which they spread upon the table I provided. They produced a number of odd trinkets and instruments: fat candles, jagged knives, pincers and the like, as well as a coil of rope. In the centre of the table, they erected a rectangular mirror. They arranged this so that while I took their picture, the mirror would capture me taking it. It was a strange arrangement, but the money was good, and I was assured that we'd deal with the demon problem as soon as the project was complete.

They sat quiet and still for their picture, then insisted that I develop the image at once. I hurried to oblige them, and whilst I worked in the darkness I heard furniture screeching across the room as they prepared it for whatever they intended. A ritual perhaps, to destroy or banish the demons I had exposed. Though how ropes and knives might become weapons against incorporeal creatures I had no idea.

I had not expected the photograph to reveal anything extraordinary. Thus far the demonic faces had appeared only in images captured in crowds, and three men and a photographer hardly constituted a crowd. Yet, as the shapes and forms began to appear, I realised that there was something strange about the picture. The three men sat perfectly composed around their table, not a blurred face to be seen, but in the mirror light shimmered and broke as though caught in rippling waves, forming the faces I had seen only in shadow before. They surrounded me, either side and above my shoulders, all leering at the lens. That long face with the protruding tongue perched grinning where my own head would have been, were I not stooped behind the camera.

My first urge was to rip the picture into pieces too small to reveal the truth of the image, but as it was not yet fixed a finer notion occurred to me. By careful application of chemicals, I could destroy only the offensive part, and so I did. There was something immensely satisfying about watching that mirror fade to impenetrable black.

I thought myself very clever as I took the picture to show my waiting clients, but stepping into the room the air around me seemed to shift and tilt. I looked down to see a large symbol daubed in black upon the floor. An enormous eye, a line through its centre. It seemed fixed on me, and I had to close my eyes against it, knees buckling beneath me.

Hands caught me by the shoulders, and the picture was torn from my grasp. I couldn't catch my breath to complain and was too weak to resist. Someone pushed me into a chair, and pulled rope tight around my legs and wrists.

"We will exorcise your demons," they said, "one way or another."

I opened my eyes, but could not see the men for all the ghastly faces, everywhere, filling my vision. I knew then, that even if the society men managed to banish every one, I would never forget those knowing eyes and forked tongues. Those images would be fixed forever in my memory.

The Hunter's Child

Amelia Brunskill

Amelia Brunskill is a writer and a librarian. Her short fiction has appeared in Indiana Review, Ninth Letter, and Arts & Letters. She has published one young adult novel, The Window, and her second one, Wolfpack, is scheduled to come out in 2022.

Miles beyond the castle, beyond this small cabin in the woods, there's a wall. I've been told that on the other side there roam monsters—hideous beasts whose roars make the ground quake, whose fangs can flay the skin from your flesh. They are what I was taught to fear, not small cabins containing too little furniture and too many empty bottles.

It seems that my education had holes in it.

The Queen should be looking for me, sending out soldiers on horseback. I should not be that difficult to find, not for someone with an army under her control.

But every day I look less like the King, and more like him, the Hunter.

He thinks that means something she can no longer deny, but it appears she'd prefer for me to stay hidden.

***

Once upon a time, I thought of the snow outside as fragile, gentle. Then he took away my shoes after the second time I tried to run back to the castle, and I learned the truth: on bare feet, it's harsh as knives.

I've toyed with the idea of trying to win my shoes back by refusing to eat or drink until he returns them. But I worry he'll call my bluff and I'll be betrayed by my own hunger. I'm not even sure if he still has them, or if they are already buried deep in the woods.

He himself owns only a single pair of heavy work boots. He keeps them with him at all times, tucking them under his bed when he sleeps.

***

He is out hunting when there is a sharp smash against the window, powerful enough to rattle the glass. When I go to the window, I find a raven lying on the sill, its wing twisted, its eyes bright and panicked.

I gather its body into a cardboard box. The raven caws weakly and jerks its head. I try to calm it by singing it an old lullaby, one sung to me a long, long time ago—not by her and not, of course, by him, but by a woman who once held me tight, wiped tears from my cheeks. I wonder where that woman is now. I wonder if I am ever in her thoughts.

***

I conceal the raven in a small drawer, taking it out to feed it only when the Hunter leaves the cabin. He would not like to have another creature sharing this small space, even one whose presence is intended to be purely temporary.

The raven like oats and raisins, I've found. It also likes fatty pieces of meat. It probably likes anything and everything that can be digested—any calories that will help it survive.

It's smart, this bird, and it stays quiet most of the time—all of the time when the Hunter is inside. Its initial suspicion of me quickly melts away, and it becomes trusting, eating whatever I give it without question, and almost, in its own avian way, affectionate.

I wonder if it has seen the monsters beyond the wall, if it has flown low to the ground and swept over their backs as they rest.

One day I wonder this aloud, and then await the raven's response. It blinks and rustles its wings.

I've become someone who talks to birds.

**

The raven heals quickly, it seems. I want to feel responsible for that, to know that I've done the right thing. Possibly I did, or possibly it would have healed on its own and I've only been selfish in keeping it here with me as long as I have. It's easy, I think, to tell yourself that you are doing the right thing. That the ends will justify the means.

I explain to it that I'm setting it free, that it should be more careful of glass, of windows, in the future. That it should not overexert its wing, take it slow. Does it take it in with a solemn expression, or do I detect a hint of a rolled eye? I imagine for myself a drawn-out farewell scene when I open the window, with hesitant glances and some tentative wing flaps with its feet still firmly gripping the windowsill, but as soon as the window is open the raven flies off, without a backward glance. I try not to be jealous of its wings flexing against the air, of how it can soar above the trees and disappear into the sky.

**

The next morning, when the sun has yet to rise above the horizon, I make coffee for the Hunter. He likes it dark and bitter, untainted by milk or sugar. After I pour it for him, I return to the counter where I begin pocketing granola for the raven before remembering it is gone.

Through a stab of what I'm afraid is disappointment, the Hunter tells me he'll be out all day, that he hopes to bring back a deer. I imagine a carcass hanging from a nearby tree, its blood pooling on the snow. It will feed us for a long time, a deer, yet the way his mood lifts at the prospect of the hunt, his calm certainty that it will go his way, means that the meat will not rest easily in my stomach.

He tells me to be good while he's away and then adds that he loves me. I wonder if he really believes that I am something other than a pawn in a game of chess she's refusing to play.

***

He's been gone for less than an hour when there is a sound at the window, a sharp rap—decisive, intentional. From across the room, I see a quick flash of black feathers.

Left on the windowsill are three things: a tuff of golden fur, a long metallic tooth, and a bright blue flower.

I stare at them for a minute before I raise the window and carefully pick them up, one by one. I have never seen an animal that the fur or the tooth might belong to, and I have also never seen a flower like that before. It makes me wonder what else I have not seen, what else there might be to discover.

***

More snow falls. Inches, then feet. The Hunter doesn't leave the house for over a week. The deer carcass is coated with snow, and soon the patches of crimson below it are subsumed by the white.

He makes stew, and even after hours, the meat remains tough and stringy. I eat it quietly, without comment, and he talks about her, the Queen.

About how she stole me from him, about how one day the three of us will be a family.

I do not question why he wants us to be a family, what that word means to him. I don't ask whether he pictures her here, or himself in the castle. Neither of them, I think, care to think too much about what happens next, about the logical consequences of their actions.

***

Early on the first morning after the snow has stopped falling, he finally leaves. There is still plenty of meat on the deer, but he wants rabbit this time.

Not long after he departs, there is another peck against glass, another flash of feathers.

Left on the windowsill this time are a small red cluster of berries.

Even very small children are taught that consuming unfamiliar fruits is a version of Russian roulette, its outcomes unknown and potentially lethal. Without even pausing to close the window, I place two berries on my tongue and swallow them whole.

***

When I open my eyes, it's getting dark outside. There's a dry tartness at the back of my throat and I'm lying crumpled beneath the open window, the remaining berries glistening on the sill.

I've lost almost a full day.

I close the window to stop the wind rushing in, and I tuck the berries into my pocket.

***

When the Hunter comes back, he asks why the house is so cold.

I say something about burning a slice of bread on the stove and opening the window to clear out the smoke. I say it too quickly and add too much detail. He does not ask again, only looks at me with hard eyes until I have to look away. He has a very good sense of smell and the air does not hold even the faintest trace of smoke.

***

When he next leaves, I stand at the windowsill and look outside.

I think about boots and fur and berries.

I place a handful of granola on the sill and mouth a wish. I wait all day, but when the dark comes, the granola remains on the sill. I brush it off onto the snow outside so that it doesn't raise questions I'm not sure if I even know how to answer.

When he returns, it is with a hammer and a box of nails.

***

He starts with the windows in back, nailing them shut. He says it's to keep out the draft, that we'll both be able to sleep better at night that way, stop shivering underneath our respective blankets. It is cold at night, there is a draft that snakes through the small cabin. Still, I can't help thinking of a friend I once had who captured a butterfly and put it in a jar, forgetting to put airholes in the lid before screwing it on so very, very tight.

***

A sharp sound heralds the arrival of berries and a soft nest of golden fur, left on the sill of the only window that has not yet been nailed shut. It's a lot of fur, enough that its original owner might have been displeased to part with it.

This time, when the raven leaves the sill, it lands on the snow only a few yards away. It stares at me, long and hard, its beady eyes asking me a question.

I answer it with a nod.

***

The next morning, I make the Hunter his coffee, dark and bitter. When he looks away for a moment, I squeeze into it the juice of four berries. He is much larger than I am, after all.

I serve it to him with my left hand, hiding the purpled skin of my right where the juice has sunk in. I try not to watch too closely as he brings the cup to his lips. I worry that four was not enough. I could have, should have, put in more.

After he's downed half his coffee, seemingly with no effect, I feel a tug of despair, certain I've made a mistake and that I won't get a chance to correct it. Then he suddenly puts down his cup, his hand unsteady. He looks surprised, like a stranger has appeared in the room, like he's been asked an unexpected question.

Perhaps I should say something as the look of surprise ebbs away and his eyes become unfocused, or as he starts to slide down in his chair.

I find I don't have anything I want to say.

***

His bootlaces are double knotted, and it takes time to undo them, and then to ease the boots from his feet. I pause for a moment, and then I take his socks as well—they are coarse wool and still warm from his body.

His boots I carefully pad with the golden fur.

They are still too large, but they'll stay on my feet. I will not be able to run fast, but I will have plenty of time to get far away from here, and the snow is falling thickly and will cover my tracks.

There is kerosene that the Hunter uses for the lamps. There are matches. I let these facts play in my mind for a moment—perhaps even more than one—before I decide, no, that's not who I want to be.

**

Outside, the raven is waiting on a branch.

It flies off, and I take a deep breath—the cold air spiking my lungs—and then I follow.

This time, I walk rather than run. After all, it's going to be a long day.

A long walk towards other monsters.

The Tiger Who Fell In Love With The Sky

Kathleen Chadwick

Kathleen Chadwick is a theatre junkie and professor living outside of Boston, Massachusetts.

Once upon a time, in the great jungles of the east, there was a tiger. He was a grand and fearsome beast, and he loved nothing in the whole world except his own self. Every morning he slept on a wide rock overlooking a pond, every evening he spent hours admiring his reflection in the water, and every night he went into the jungle and killed something for his dinner. When he snarled the animals of the jungle shivered in fear, but when he walked he was so silent that they never noticed him until it was too late, his hot breath was on their back and his sharp teeth at their neck.

One evening as the tiger was gazing at his reflection in the pond below his rock, lost in admiration of his own gold-green eyes, he felt something strike him on the rump. Most offended by this interruption of his evening's contemplation, he looked all around himself until he found an unripe fig on the ground. Imagining it must have fallen from the fig tree which shaded his rock from the heat of the day, he lay back down and commenced to consider the symmetrical perfection of his many stripes. Shortly, though, he felt another fig hit him on the rump, followed by a second, and a third, and then a veritable rain of unripe fruits. "This has never happened before," he thought to himself, "in all the years I've been sleeping under this tree." And then he heard a sort of chittering laughter coming from high above him.

Looking up into the branches of the tree, he saw, almost at the very top, a small brown monkey. The monkey was eating figs.

When he came across an unripe one, he would throw it at the tiger. His aim was distressingly accurate.

"What do you think you're doing?" snarled the tiger. "If you throw one more fig at me, I'll climb up there and eat you whole!"

"You can't climb up here," said the monkey, "You couldn't get halfway up here without the limbs breaking under your fat ass."

The tiger could see that the beastly little creature was right. While he did not consider himself to be in any manner of speaking "fat", the branches at the top of the tree were barely strong enough to hold up the tiny monkey, much less a noble personage such as himself.

"You wouldn't be worth it anyway," he said, lying back down on his rock. "Too scrawny to make a meal of."

"You didn't think that about my mother," said the monkey. "You ate my mother and you ate my father and you ate all my sisters and you ate all my brothers."

"That is the way of the jungle," said the tiger. "If you didn't eat those figs they might grow into trees, but you're eating them all and so the tree will never have offspring."

"I know," said the monkey, "I know. I don't try to work against it. I just content myself with sitting here and throwing figs at your striped self and laughing at you every chance I get."

The tiger decided that continuing this conversation would be beneath his dignity. He returned to the silent meditation of his whiskers, ignoring the occasional impact of an unripe fig on his sleek backside.

As the sun was finally setting, the monkey spoke again, and this time his voice was much closer. The tiger looked up to see him on the lowest branch of the tree, almost within reach of one of the tiger's great and deadly paws.

"You think you got it all figured out," said the monkey, "but you ain't. You eat and you sleep and you stare at your precious nose in the pond, but you don't have anything figured out."

"What do you mean?" asked the tiger, most affronted.

"You got no love," said the monkey. "You've got nobody but yourself. And you think that's okay now, but love is gonna find you one day, and you're not prepared for that. Love is gonna find you and kick your ass."

"I have no idea what you're talking about," said the tiger coldly.

"I know you don't," said the monkey.

"I imagine I will have no trouble finding a mate when I desire one," said the tiger.

"That's not what I'm talking about," said the monkey, and he ran off into the tree, then leapt to another and disappeared into the jungle.

The tiger was somewhat disturbed by this conversation. That night he was distracted while he stalked the forest and ended up catching no dinner for himself at all. He returned to his rock and threw himself down upon it. Instead of going to sleep on a full stomach, as was his usual habit, he gazed at his moonlit reflection in the pond. He lay there, staring deeply and disconsolately into his own eyes, later than he had ever been awake before. So late, in fact, that it became not late at all, but very, very early instead. As the sun rose, which the tiger had never seen before, he noticed for the first time that the pond reflected something besides himself.

The sky was the lightest of blues, pink at the eastern horizon, and streaks of clouds were blazing gold from north to south. The tiger had never seen anything so beautiful in his life. His own stripes seemed pale and dingy in comparison and his eyes muddy and dim. He rolled onto his back to see the sky itself, but the sight seemed to burn his eyes and heart. He was able to stare only at the reflection in the pond.

The tiger watched the sky's reflection all that day. He watched all night. He watched the next dawn and thought it more beautiful than the one before. He watched as the sun journeyed across his pond and marveled at its brightness. He watched the progression of blues and then pinks and then more blues and blacks as the days and nights passed. The stars, so much brighter than his own eyes, entranced him.

He did not eat. He did not wash himself. He did not sleep.

On the third day, the monkey came to him again.

"I know what you mean now," said the tiger, when he noticed the monkey in the tree.

"Yes, I expect you do," said the monkey. He looked at the dusty, rumpled, red-eyed tiger. "You look like shit."

"Is that satisfying?" asked the tiger.

"Pretty satisfying, yeah," said the monkey.

"What do I do now?" asked the tiger.

"Well, have you told her?" asked the monkey. "That's usually the first step."

"No," said the tiger.

"Who is she?" asked the monkey. "I haven't seen any lady tigers around."

"I'm not in love with a tiger," said the tiger. "I think I've fallen in love with the sky."

"The sky!" whooped the monkey. "This is better than I thought! You love the sky? You hit the bad-luck jackpot, man. You never gonna be happy again! You should just sit on that rock and let yourself starve to death now, 'cause you're never gonna get the sky to love you back."

"Why not?" said the tiger. "Am I not handsome and strong and sleek?"

"Not after staying up for three days straight, no," said the monkey, "but that's not the point. It's *the sky*. It don't love nobody, just like you."

"I changed," said the tiger, "so can the sky. I've watched her change constantly for three days and nights, actually."

"Sky can't change like that," said the monkey. "But I tell you what. There's a monkey. A very wise old monkey. Lives in a cave. He might know how to get the sky to talk to you. He knows lots of things. So you go to him and see what he says."

"Why are you helping me?" asked the tiger suspiciously. "I ate your whole family."

"I'm not helping you," said the monkey. "If you think helping you talk to the sky 'cause you're in love with it is *helping you*, you still got a lot to learn."

"All right," said the tiger. "How do I find the wise monkey?"

The monkey gave him directions to the cave where the wise old monkey lived. It was across a river and through a jungle, and through the territory of a herd of elephants, which even tigers fear, and across another river, and through a swamp, and then right at another river, and up a great mountain. "And bring some figs," said the monkey. "He likes figs, and it never hurts to take figs when you're going to visit a monkey."

"I will," said the tiger. "Thank you."

"Don't thank me," said the monkey. "I'm hoping you get stepped on by the elephants."

The tiger finally slept that day, and caught himself a dinner that night, and the next night he left for the mountain. He walked all night and slept in trees on his trip. The first river was small; he barely got his chin wet. He crossed the elephants' ground in one night, slinking from shadow to shadow. He saw the huge animals sleeping, like hills with trees for legs, but he was so silent that none of them woke. The second river was wild and cold, coming down from the mountains. He was sick for two days after crossing it. The swamp left him filthy, covered in mud and bug bites. He swam in the third river to clean himself before turning upstream and starting to climb the mountain. Nearing dawn, he found a fig tree and carefully gathered the ripest figs he could reach. He wrapped them in a leaf and gently carried the bundle in his mouth up the mountain until he came to a cave. There was a broad open space out front of the cave, and here he set down the figs and called for the wise monkey.

"I'm not coming down there," came a voice from the forest. "You say you came here looking for a wise monkey, how wise would I be to come when a tiger calls for me?"

"I'm not going to eat you," said the tiger. "I've brought you figs. Besides, after coming all this way to see you, I must be a sorry sight myself. I can barely stand, much less chase down a monkey. I've been walking for weeks." And this was true, as the wise monkey could see. The tiger was thin. His bright eyes were tired and his stripes faded under a layer of dust.

The monkey came down from his tree, out into the clearing. He sniffed the figs. "What is it you want, then?" he asked, examining a fig.

"I'm in love with the sky. I want to meet her. A monkey told me you could get her to talk to me," said the tiger.

"Hmph. That monkey has an inflated idea of my abilities," said the wise old monkey, now munching contentedly on a fig. "Good figs, though."

"Oh," said the tiger. "Is there nothing you can do to help me?"

"Well, I can try. I'm not promising anything, mind."

"Whatever you can do, I will appreciate it."

After considering for a time, and eating three more figs, the monkey told the tiger, "Go into my cave. Touch nothing you see there, it is monkey magic. Go all the way to the back. There are two passageways. Take the right one. At every fork you come to, go right. You will travel through tunnels, all the way through the mountain. They get smaller as you go, and I'm not sure you'll be able to squeeze through, skinny though you are for a tiger. If you make it, you will come out onto a little ledge on the other side of the mountain." Here the monkey fell silent for a long time.

"And then what do I do?" asked the tiger.

"Do? Nothing. You wait. If the sky will talk to you, that's where it will happen," said the monkey.

The tiger was not inspired to confidence by this plan. "What if I get trapped in the passageway?" he asked.

"Well," said the monkey," I expect one of two things will happen then. If you're only trapped a little, you'll sit there until you get thinner and thinner and then you'll be able to wiggle free and move further along."

"And if I can't move further along?" asked the tiger.

The old monkey smiled. "Then I'll have some tiger bones to add to my monkey magic in the cave," he said.

There seemed to be no more to say. Nodding his thanks to the monkey, the tiger left the bright morning behind as he entered the cave. The walls of the cave were carved into shelves, and they were covered with bones and sticks and twists of jungle grasses right up to the top. The tiger passed these by carefully, avoiding touching them or even looking too closely. At the back of the cave, there were two openings, and he took the one on the right. For many hours he walked through the dark passage beneath the mountain, taking the right path at every fork. He sometimes thought he heard things, monkey laughter and singing. Sometimes sparks seemed to fly in front of his eyes in the dark. The tunnels grew smaller and smaller and twisted in strange ways. Once he thought he had made a wrong turn and come to a dead end, but then he saw that the passage twisted back on top of itself, and he hauled himself up, crawling now only a few feet above where he had been a moment ago. He was stuck for a time which seemed infinitely long, but probably was not. He imagined himself dying here in the darkness and the old monkey cackling as he carried him back to the cave, pieces of tiger-bone-monkey-magic. With some scrabbling he worked himself free.

At last he noticed it was getting brighter, and though the tunnel was smaller than ever, he squeezed himself towards the brightness. He emerged from the cave onto a tiny ledge. He now saw that the other side of the mountain was a sheer cliff. He was most of the way up, and the drop was terrifying. Instead of looking straight down at the rocks and the deadly fall, he looked out on the valley in front of him.

It was sunset, and the light was golden across the valley. The tiger could see the jungle stretching far away, covering hills and valleys and mountains. He heard faintly the calls of distant birds and saw treetops shaking as packs of monkeys moved through them. Finally the tiger looked up at his love, the sky. She seemed closer than ever, and she was in tiger stripes again, golden orange and blue. Far above everything, the tiger felt that he was with his love, living in the sky. Exhausted from his journey, he fell asleep.

In the night he dreamed. He dreamed of looking and watching over the jungle and the ocean and the world beyond. He dreamed of towns and cities. He dreamed of clouds and winds. He dreamed of the feelings of pink and red and deepest blue. Finally, he dreamed of watching himself, lying on a ledge. In the last dream he was both watching over himself and in his own body, feeling a presence near him.

He woke in the morning, alone. He was weak from his long weeks of walking, and to go back through the cave seemed too hard. "I will wait here until the sky comes to speak to me," he decided. "She surely came to me in my dreams last night, for I've never had such dreams before. If I wait, she may come again."

He waited all day, watching the valley and the sky above it. Now that he was frail, she did not seem to blind him as before, but to comfort him. He waited this way through three days, watching the light and the sky in the day and dreaming of them and the presence beside him each night. It was cold on the side of the mountain and wet with dew in the mornings. He grew weaker.

"I could not walk back through the mountain now if I wanted to," he realized on the fourth morning. "I will die here on this ledge. The monkey will take my bones and use them for his purposes, and I will be forgotten in the jungle." The thought did not disturb him as much as he thought it might. He was living in the sky, or as near as he could come to her. He dozed on and off all through the day, dreaming in bright blues. In the evening, he was awake and watched the sun set. He wanted to watch the stars again. As the sunset faded into darkness and the stars shone through the veil of the last light, he saw a form moving towards him through the sky. The figure came closer and he saw that it was a she-tiger, striped with deepest blue and brightest orange, glowing with the last of the day's light. The she-tiger walked across the sky and came to the ledge where the tiger lay. She sat next to him, not on the ledge, but in the sky beside it.

"Are you the sky?" he asked.

The she-tiger shook her great head and smiled. "I am not the whole sky. I am that part of the sky which is a tiger. The whole sky cannot come down to love one tiger. But I have seen how you love me, with great constancy. I have watched over you the past three nights."

"Will you be with me while I die?" asked the tiger.

The sky-tiger smiled again. "Only if you wish to die," she said. "If you wish to live, you shall do that instead, and I will live with you."

The tiger was surprised to find that, given a choice, he still wanted to live. He nodded to the sky-tiger, and she picked him up by the back of the neck like a cub and carried him through the mountain. Where the passage was tight she shrugged her shoulders and it widened for them. After a time, carried rocking through the darkness, the tiger fell asleep. When he awoke he was outside the cave and the sky-tiger was talking to the monkey. The monkey gave the sky-tiger a twist of grass. She lay down on the ground quietly and allowed the monkey to pluck from her face a single pale blue whisker. The monkey grinned over his prize and retreated to his cave. The sky-tiger brought the twist of grass to the tiger and put it in his jaws. It was dry and sharp. The tiger ate it carefully.

"Better?" asked the sky-tiger.

"Somewhat," said the tiger, managing to stand.

The journey which had taken the tiger four weeks alone took them twice that together. It took them two weeks to reach the place where the tiger had first met the river and turned up the mountain. The sky-tiger hunted and brought prey back to the tiger to eat each night, and he gained strength as they went. The wind seemed always to favor the sky-tiger, and she was silent as the faintest breeze. She was a remarkably good hunter, though she shone a little under the starlight.

The two tigers hunted and lived together for many years. They had fine litters of cubs and watched them grow into great and fearsome tigers. The children were the orange-and-black of their father, but at night the faint glow of starshine rose from their hides. Parents and children were the terror of the jungle, though none of them ate monkeys again.

One autumn morning, after they had watched the sunrise from the rock overlooking the pond, the tiger said to his love, "You will return to the sky soon."

The sky-tiger said, "I will be with you all your life."

"I am not young," said the tiger. "Winter is coming, and I do not think I will see the spring."

"I have lived with you here for a long time," said the sky-tiger. " Perhaps it is time for you to come and live in my home."

"I cannot walk in the sky as you can, my love," said the tiger.

They slept that day, and in the evening they left the rock for the last time. Again they crossed rivers and the grounds of the elephants and the swamp. They walked together up the mountain, but the wise monkey was not at his cave, and the objects inside were dusty and jumbled.

"He was a very old monkey, even when I was young," said the tiger, and he was a little sad, though he had not liked the monkey.

They crept together through the passageways. It was easier this time, for the tiger was shrunken a little with age, and the places where the sky-tiger had shrugged her shoulders were still enlarged.

The ledge was as it had been years before, perched between earth and sky.

"From here you must walk alone," said the tiger. "Come to me at night, as you did when we first met, and I will be waiting."

"I will," said the sky-tiger, and she left the little ledge and walked into the sky.

She came back that night, and stayed with him until the sky was pink at the edges and the sun was about to rise. "My love," she said. "Come with me to my home."

"I cannot live in the sky," said the tiger. "When I was young and arrogant I thought to love the whole sky, but now I love only you and that is enough, and more."

"Once before I gave you a choice," said the sky-tiger. "Now I give it to you again. When you were young you loved the sky so much that I came down to be with you. Now I love you. Will you not come to live with me?"

The tiger considered this. He rose, and followed her into the sky.

Ghosts in My Lungs

Madeleine Sardina

Madeleine Sardina is a writer of all things weird and magical. She's been published in Psychopomp Magazine, The New Southern Fugitives, 45th Parallel, and elsewhere. She's also the author of the fiction collection Lonely Creatures. She can be found in grainy photographs taken in the forests of the Rocky Mountains or online @mgsardina.

I met her in the refrigerated section. In the dead of summer, I was the coldest thing around and she found me with five pounds of chicken in each hand and a plastic bag of tomatoes tucked under my arm. "Do you need help?"

I looked at her, sweat shining off the tops of her shoulders and dark strands of hair clinging to her forehead, and felt that first heatwave like I'd just walked outside. "Oh, I'm okay, I—"

She eased the tomatoes out from my armpit. "Didn't think you'd need a basket?"

Her eyebrow arched up toward her bangs, a smile teased at her lips, and I wanted to crawl between the piles of cured meats or cartons of milk rather than answer her. "It—" A deep breath in. "I'm just making a dinner run."

"You're making ten pounds of chicken for dinner?" she asked, and the smile came out then, sizzling across the plastic-wrapped chicken.

"No."

I dropped one package back onto the shelf, my eyes flickering from her face for only a second, and then held my hand out for the tomatoes. She held them back, a challenging tilt to her jaw. "You'll have the same problem again soon enough if you don't get a basket," she said.

I felt the heat radiating from her even in this chilled section of the store, steaming through her tank and running shorts. The chill that lived inside me twisted, but the rest of me moved toward her, orbiting her shyly, and handed her the remaining chicken. "Thank you," I said, and in the shared space between us, the ghosts that lived inside me fogged the air.

They stayed in my lungs most often, sunk low and heavy. Sometimes they sifted through my veins like venom, cold and blue, raising goosebumps as they went. Sometimes they slipped out in coughs and sneezes, or icy words, but they always slinked back in, liquid frost dripping down my throat. They don't speak, not in their own voices, but still I can hear them like the crunch of packed snow or the crack of ice on a frozen lake. I keep my lips shut tight when I can, to contain them, to keep from spilling their chill into my own words.

I found that difficult the day I met her. "Don't you have your own shopping to do?" I asked her as I searched for balsamic vinegar.

"No," she said, still holding my chicken and tomatoes. "I came in for the air conditioning."

I stood from my squat on the ground, coming back up with balsamic and olive oil. She held her open hand out for the bottles. The sweat on her shoulders was dry but in the creases of her skin it still glistened. "This is all I need," I lied. "I can take it. Thank you."

"No basil?" she asked. "Mozzarella?" She tilted her head and the fluorescent light reflected against the damp skin of her neck.

"No," I said. "I'm not making— no." My teeth ached like I'd taken a bite of ice cream.

"Okay," she said. Only then did she withdraw her open palm,

but still she didn't return the chicken and tomatoes. "I can carry these to checkout with you."

The ghosts pressed against my lips, solid in their violence, and I knew if I opened my mouth they would devour her. So I turned, silent, and she followed me.

Outside, the summer heat was brilliant and the ghosts dripped back into my chest. "Thank you," I said, when she finally handed over my bag of groceries.

"Do you want to get smoothies?" she asked. She pushed her hair off her forehead, tugged a scrunchy from her wrist, bound back the thick black hair that stubbornly clung to her skin. I said nothing, and she continued. "Or coffee? It's a little hot, but—"

"Okay."

"Okay! You live close?"

I gestured up the road with a nod. "Great! You know The Drip on Main? Drop your things off and I'll meet you there."

"Now?"

"Unless you're busy."

She was sitting by the window when I met her twenty minutes later, sipping on an iced vanilla latte. I sat across from her, curled my hands around my mug of hot chocolate. "You don't like whipped cream?" she asked.

"No."

"Why?"

I took a gulp of the steaming liquid, felt the roof of my mouth blister, sending the ghosts back deep into my diaphragm. They fussed, filled what cracks they could between my organs, but stayed down, down, down. "Too cold," I said.

She did most of the talking, her hands making fluttering shapes in front of her as she told me about herself—her job as a rock climbing instructor, her brother who was also her roommate, her favorite books and movies and the classes she was taking sporadically at the community college. "I'm not looking for a degree," she said with a vague wave, like she was brushing away a fly. "I just like learning, so I take whatever classes I think look cool. If that included any math I'd probably have, like, four degrees by now."

My hot chocolate was long gone, but I still kept my hands wrapped around the mug. The ghosts were slowly seeping back into my veins, restless and tangible. "How about you?" she asked, rattling her straw around her cup even after all the ice had melted. "Are you studying anything?"

"English."

"Nice! Literature is one of my favorite subjects. Can I try to guess your favorite writer?"

She reached across the table and I swallowed hard, forced down the riotous ghosts, held my breath to keep them in place. She gently (so gently I trembled with it) pulled my fingers from their place on the chilled ceramic of my mug. Her hand was warm like a freshly drawn bath, like laundry pulled straight from the dryer, like the end of winter. She touched me like she was afraid she might burn me, with just the tips of her fingers dancing between my thumb and forefinger, and when I did not snatch my hand back, she clasped me tighter. "Frost."

She waited weeks to kiss me. I could've kissed her first, but the last time I had kissed someone, the ghosts had poured from my mouth into theirs and we'd both come away coughing. I was so afraid of choking her. So I waited, as we both stood outside her apartment one June evening, hands clasped, loitering because I had to go home and she had to go to bed, but the cicadas' song was too lovely to leave. When I finally unlaced my fingers from hers, when the ghosts swept in and turned my fingernails blue, she stretched up onto her tiptoes and kissed my cheek. "Oh," she whispered, sounding wounded. Her hand reached up, hovered uncertainly over the place her lips had just been. "Oh no, it's red. Did it burn?"

I rubbed the spot, trying to find a blister or a scorch mark with my fingertips. There was so much fear in her wide brown eyes as she looked up at me, and I knew it was the fear she saw in me whenever I opened my mouth and prayed the ghosts would let me speak. "No," I said, and it was true. She was so warm but she never burned me. "No, it's fine. You can—"

She took my face in her hands and pulled me down, kissed me so soundly I only had to hug her waist and hold on.

***

She was never cold. "Never ever," she said, and she looked so sad when she told me while we lay on her bed, the window wide open and the curtains drifting in the summer breeze.

She was sprawled on top of me, chin sharp against my breastbone but I couldn't find it in myself to mind. Her legs and arms were matched to mine and we must've looked ridiculous, frozen in some kind of mirror exercise, but everywhere her skin touched mine was a place the ghosts couldn't hide. I hadn't told her this. Instead, I'd said, "My hands are cold. My arms are cold. My legs now." By the time every inch of her was pressed to me she was laughing so hard her cheeks glowed. She pressed her smile to my neck, slid her fingers in between mine, and when she began to kiss beneath my jaw, I felt a flicker of heat inside myself.

There were days her heat burned brighter, too bright for her to leave her apartment. She would call me, gasping, choking on the heat that bubbled up inside her. The first time, I brought ice and smoothies, the ghosts running wild inside me. They were quieter in the summer, weaker, but they drew cold from the things I held and filled my body with it. I was shivering on her doorstep, holding the bag of ice out when her brother opened the door.

He was quieter than her, but just as kind in the way he asked how I was and offered me some iced tea while he took the cold things I'd brought. "Iced tea?" I asked, but the ghosts made me spit it, vile and sarcastic. My teeth clattered together. "Are you kidding?"

Before he could respond, two arms, burnished bronze and damp with sweat, wrapped around my waist. She slid her hands beneath my shirt and I thought foolishly for a moment that perhaps she was a bit feverish. Her palms pressed to my stomach, her cheek between my shoulder blades, and the ghosts quailed against her heat. I ran my hands along her arms, gently, shyly, still. "Did you bring ice?" she asked, and through the exhaustion and slur of her speech, I heard a smile.

"You said you were hot."

She hummed in response and her brother held up the smoothie and a cup of ice in each hand. I saw the way he held them at arms reach, the way he winced when she reached towards him, and I knew there must be some wave radiating from her that he couldn't bear, that I couldn't feel. She took the ice, tipped it back into her mouth, chomped on the shards. Steam poured out of her nostrils—not the same heavy fog I choked on when my ghosts were loud, but like a teakettle or a dragon. The moisture clung to my skin, dripped down my nose, and I swept my tongue over my upper lip. She watched me, took my hand, pulled me back to her room.

Her bedsheets, as well as her thin camisole and running shorts, were soaked through with sweat already, but when she pulled me against her on the bed I went so, so willingly. She was crooning some heat-made language, nonsense created by the fever, but I heard every plea when she pressed her lips to my ear. "Hold," she said, and I did, stripping down and folding myself around her. The ghosts pooled in my core, furious, unable to fight against her scorching skin.

She lay curled in my arms while her insides boiled, sometimes sleeping, sometimes sobbing quietly into my chest, sometimes babbling as if she were drunk, as if this was all a dream. "I will pour you out," she murmured, forehead pressed to mine while she wrapped my long hair around both our heads like a web, a cocoon. "I will pour you into a glass, a frozen glass! And I will drink you."

"Have to be a pretty tall glass."

She cackled, long and manic, and then kissed me like she really would gulp me down.

Each time the fever blazed, I stayed like this with her. It would fade eventually, usually by the next morning and I would wake with clammy skin, chilled, knowing it was past.

By the end of August, her fevers had mellowed. "Summer is ending," she told me one evening when I noted she hadn't had one in two weeks. "They only happen in summer, when the heat inside me can't escape." She played with my fingers idly, curling them around her own in silly shapes. "Except with you. It doesn't even get to escape with you, it just...melts."

I wanted to tell her she had it backwards, that she would have to melt me when the weather cooled, that I could already feel the ghosts turning me to stone when the sun went down. But she had said it so softly, like even she was unsure, that I couldn't find a way to dispute her. So I only kissed her forehead and let her press her nose to my clavicle.

I began to dream of fires—infernos that worked their way inwards towards me as I stood on a darkened highway. I saw the flames approaching on each side, sparks arching above me, spiraling onto the asphalt and sputtering out at my feet. The heat didn't reach me but the glow set my skin alight. I always woke shivering and coughing, my chilled breath steaming the air around me. The ghosts never let the warmth keep me long.

It was early fall when I thought I would lose her, finally. Earlier than I had hoped, but the first frost was always a surprise. I awoke shivering, buried beneath my mountain of blankets, and felt the ghosts in my marrow, in every bone. I thought I might snap in half if I moved.

She called at noon and I did not answer. She called again at dinner and again I did not answer. The ghosts were so thick inside me I imagined them carving away my insides to make more room. I cranked the space heater as high as it would go, mounded my blankets higher until there were none left, brewed pot after pot of tea and then eventually only hot water, pouring the nigh-boiling liquid directly from the kettle down my throat, and still the ghosts howled. When the fever had come over her, she had called me and begged for company. When my chill came, I could not open my mouth for fear of releasing all the vile things inside me.

I heard the front door unlock well past sundown. The cold kept me hidden in my nest, or more likely the fear, but still she found me. "Oh love," she sighed, her voice muffled through the fabric.

The ghosts raged at the simple sound of her voice. Like grease on a flame, they blazed up, and I shuddered so violently the blankets billowed off of me. "Who let you in?" I growled. My voice was distant, detached from my own ears, and I would have cowered from myself.

"I have your spare key," she reminded me gently.

"Leave."

She stood there, rooted, no step forward but no step away. I yanked on the blankets and only then noticed she was holding them tight in one fist. "Give them back," I snapped, my voice breaking like a shard of glass on the last word.

"Are you cold?" she asked, and I knew, I knew, she did not ask it facetiously, she did not mean to ask the obvious. She only wanted to find a way in, a break in my armor where she could reach me. But the ghosts have never been very forgiving. I have never been very forgiving.

"Am I cold?"

The icy mist poured from my mouth, my nose, out my ears like something had finally burst inside me. "Why are you here?" I hissed, crawling forward on my bed. "I never asked you to come. I never invited you—I gave you a spare key in case I locked myself out. Just because you need me when you're sick doesn't mean I want the same thing. I want silence, peace, not your— your fucking attitude in my space! I don't need it! Get out— get out of m-my house!"

The ghosts whipped through the air around us, their laughter like the first crackle of thunder. They shattered the lamp's light-bulb, the space heater, every mug cluttering my bedside table. Some of them had faces—unrecognizable, but familiar, human, and they looked at both of us as if they knew us. It was difficult to look directly at them, and they moved so fast as to make it impossible anyway. "You see?" I shouted at her over their ruckus. "How am I supposed to deal with this if you're here?"

She looked away from them, back to me, her mouth hanging slightly open and her eyes wide with fear, or something similar. She'd dropped the blankets in her shock, and I snatched at them again. "Wait—"

Her sharp plea hardly preceded her leap onto the bed, and in the rush I pulled the blankets over both of us, hiding from the ghosts that raged throughout the room. Her breath filled the space beneath the blankets immediately, thick and warm and sweet like green tea. "Is this how you deal with it usually?" she asked. The darkness hid her face but I thought I heard the lilt in her voice that always accompanied her smile.

"They don't usually get out," I said. Now that the ghosts were out, my rage was melting quickly.

"Maybe now they'll leave you alone for good?"

"No," I told her. "They rarely get out but they always...always come back."

Another crash sounded above us, and something buffeted the side of our blanket fortress. She flinched, and before I could tell her again to leave my home, she crawled into my arms, all warm skin and soft, tickling strands of hair. She tucked the blanket beneath the back of my head, securing us inside this nest, and then pressed her forehead against my throat. "Fine," she sighed, and the puff of air that came with it raised goosebumps on my clavicle. "Let them try."

I was frozen against her, rigid in fear and a lingering anger. "I was handling them fine before you came."

"Were you? Because when I came in all I saw was a pile of very soft, very trembly blankets."

There was a burst of cold air beside my ear and I flinched, clutching at her. She hugged me tight, her palms slipping beneath the three sweaters I was wearing and pressing flush to my back. "This is not handling it, love," she said, not unkindly. "You shouldn't be alone in this."

We lay like that, her pressed tight against me while I trembled with fear and with the chill that would never leave me, even when the ghosts ran wild in the air around us. I knew it would abate if she pressed her bare skin to mine, if I took off all the layers of clothes I had armored myself with, but after the things that I'd said to her and with the shame of all my insides poured out, I wanted the cold to hurt. I wanted it to burn me the way I knew she never would.

Eventually, the ghosts tired themselves out. They pressed down on us in a thick fog, dampening the blanket. I knew she would never really feel their cold but I hated the thought of them touching her, so I peeled the blanket back from my face and took a deep breath. They rushed in all at once, filled my chest and pushed out further, and I coughed, choked around them. She sat up, pulled me up too, as if an upright position would settle what was inside me again. "In through your nose," she said, "out...out your mouth."

She was uncertain. They'd made her uncertain—or I had. Maybe she didn't know how welcome her advice would be now. Either way, I did as she said, made a point of it. My breath fogged the air and I clutched my arms around myself. Her hand on my back, patting idly, slid down to the many hems of my sweaters, hesitated. "Please," I breathed. I'd said this word before, when her hands toyed with my other edges, but this plea was not the same. It cracked and promised to break if she wasn't careful. But she was. She always was.

Her arms slid beneath my sweaters, wrapped tight around my waist, and held. I hugged her shoulders and trembled against her until her warmth seeped into my bones and I finally, finally, stopped shivering. The ghosts had used so much of themselves that even they couldn't find an argument against her heat. They slept inside, placated for now, and I fell into her. "Do you want to sleep?" she asked as she lowered me back onto the bed.

"I'm sorry."

"I know."

"I'm really, really sorry," I insisted. "I do this when it's cold. It's only just starting."

"I figured. Do they always get this bad?"

"Sometimes. There's never anyone around when it does. I make sure."

She pressed her forehead to mine. "Is that why you were so mad that I came? You were afraid for me?"

It would be so easy to say yes—yes, that was out of protection, that was out of concern or panic, not my own nastiness.

"No," I whispered. "I was only thinking about myself. I wasn't expecting you. I...I get so much worse when I'm cold. So much more me, concentrated me, like my core—"

"It fills your whole body," she said, not a question or a realization, but a confession.

"You're never like this with your fever."

"Not exactly like this," she allowed. "Not the same, but similar. Mine is more...in my feelings? Well, you've seen." She slid one hand out from under my sweaters and took my wrist, pulling my hand up to press flat against her breastbone. She held it there. "Not many people can say that. That they've seen me all shrieks and tears and still stuck around."

She pulled her other hand out and pressed it over our joined ones. I still felt her touch on my waist, on my back, the ghosts not yet swept back in her wake. "Do you want me to stick around?" she asked, a softness alongside the teasing lilt she uses to hide. She would leave, if I asked. But only if I asked.

"Yes."

Magpie Girls

Savannah Wade

Savannah Wade studied Creative Writing at UNC Asheville, graduating in 2016. Since then she has published several poems and a flash fiction piece titled "Small and Hidden" which won 2nd place in the One Month of Solitude Writing Competition. Currently she lives in Raleigh where she drinks too much coffee and speak to too many ghosts.

I didn't always steal beautiful things. I hopped over rocks and red and blue flower beds, holding the wooden box to my chest. I stopped to catch my breath on the green hill overlooking the pond and saw, gleefully, Lily sitting on a blanket at the far end, her face angled to the sun. I ran the length of the pond and plopped down next to her in a fit of breathlessness.

She snapped out of her peace and began giggling at my entrance.

"Jo, what is the urgency? Should I be frightened?" She asked mockingly, pulling a strand of her hair behind her ear.

I nodded, a wild look in my eyes. "Yes. When Mrs. Danfield discovers the box missing, she will surely create a secret search party."

Lily's eyes fell to where I held the box protectively in my hands.

"You took it all?" She grinned mischievously and pulled the box from me, lifting the lid.

I tucked my legs under me and sat back.

"I...It all seemed too perfect? Truly perfect and she would ruin it. She would..." I threw my hands up, trying to conjure the image. "She would burn it all and summon something terrible, something biblical!"

Lily threw her head back laughing, her pearly teeth shining.

"You are so fanciful, Miss Josephine Lemmons. Don't fret; she'll never find out who did it. She still doesn't know who stole her copy of The Great God Pan."

I reached out quickly and gripped her wrist. "You didn't..."

She smirked and refused to look at me. She always bit her thin lips before telling a secret.

"You wouldn't!"

Lily laughed wholeheartedly again and nodded. "I loved it to pieces and she wouldn't let anyone even touch it. For good reason too --it offers more education than this school in its entirety."

I put my hands under my calves and pushed my weight onto them. It certainly taught more than was recommended. I would never read such a morally repugnant book, but Lily loved to read and from every subject, even the sinful ones. Could an education like that be good for her? She was bound to find a husband as soon as school was finished. Perhaps a book was better than a man. Even Lily would agree with me on that.

"Shall we put it all in the tree?" She asked, taking out each item one by one and inspecting them carefully with a delicate touch.

I nodded, watching the tree past her shoulder. It was a looming Manchester poplar with a thick hollowed-out knot taller than us just so we could reach in and hide away our treasures. It was the most perfect tree. It sat at the furthest side of the pond that most of the other students didn't bother to explore. That also meant teachers kept their distance.

We put different things inside the knot. Lillian sought beautiful things. Torn silk ribbons, broken pieces of jewelry, and once she even found a gold coin that rolled in from the street through the gate. She began jumping holding it up so it glinted light around her like she stole the sun's attention. Lillian says gold used to be quite popular, especially in Rome. It wasn't a gold coin, at least not a Roman one, but I dared not say. I cared more for forgotten things. A piece of broken teacup, candle stubs with short wicks, and what I found yesterday, a small bust of Shakespeare with the top of his head chopped clean off. I found it under the window of Madame Dupuy's class where she probably chucked him out during class to prove one of her flourished points of poetic art and theatrical deviance.

The tree was ours and I feared the day it no longer was. We were growing so fast. My knees were still knobby and my hair a vast wasteland of braids which was Lily's feeble attempt to help me be presentable. She was no longer the child I remained. She had grown into her shoulders and chest and her hair was soft and golden. She acted as if we were the same, though clearly, we were not. I was only a year behind, but I could see decades between us.

"What is this?"

I looked up and saw her holding up a tall card. I took it from her and looked closely.

It was about the size of my hand with faded drawings of people within a thin black border. One was a young man leaning over a table covered in knives, balls, and short broken branches. Once carefully painted now worn and faded. The figure wore a large hat and gestured out of the picture with a short wand. Below him was "Le Batelevr."

"No idea. Do you know what the bottom means?"

"No, which is a real shame. What was the point of living in Paris every summer if I can't translate some mysterious card?"

"It's very odd...Maybe we should get rid of them?"

Lillian shook her head and tried to pull it out of my hand. "Oh no, these are fantastically strange things."

"You aren't suggesting..."

"Maybe they're magic?"

I laughed and collapsed onto the grass. "Magic? Certainly not... Even if they have a fearful look to them." I looked at her and realized I could see her more clearly with the rays of sun peeking through the tree limbs.

Her skin was kissed with sun, soft and speckled with freckles. Her brown eyes were always curious and demanding. Thin blonde waves blew across her face with each gentle breeze. Her nose was small and perfectly rounded. Her cheekbones struck me most, sharp under skin and never red like my own. She felt like a desired reflection, one sought after midnight somewhere dark and forbidding. However far better than my own reflection, for she was right next to me.

She rolled her eyes, letting go of the card, then looked over. Her smile dropped and her eyes widened. I turned my head around and saw Mrs. Dansfield standing with Headmistress Martin. Both stared sternly at us both, and Mrs. Dansfield, with her frizzled black hair, curled her lip at me.

"Miss Lemmons and Miss Albrecht, you both are to come with us. A discussion needs to be had," Mrs. Martins said, disappointed.

Mrs. Dansfield twitched her nose like a pig at the air and said with her top lip scrunched up and nearly touching her nostrils, "Let me talk to Ms. Albrecht. If we split them up, we can get a better idea of how this insolence occurred."

The Headmistress folded her hands and nodded sorrowfully. "Very well. Girls, come along."

I held the card to my chest and Lily held onto the box and the four of us walked back like surviving soldiers after a long battle back into the main hall.

***

The sun disappeared quickly behind a cloud and I opened my eyes to Lily standing over me. "You're alive!"

She knelt down and hugged me, her chest pressing into me.

"Of course I'm alive. Mrs. Martins wasn't going to have me hung, drawn, and quartered--"

Lily walked over to the pond's edge and looked in, placing her hands on her hips. "Mrs. Dansfield wanted blood, let me tell you. She broke the box! I've never seen a woman so full of rage. I hope I never become that."

I stood quickly. "She broke it? What a foul thing. If she is to have no goodness, then no one is."

"It was truly dreadful, Jo. She is only like that because her husband sleeps in a separate bed and takes baths in sock water."

I stifled a laugh which caused Lillian to knit her eyebrows, full of seriousness. "It is not funny...I know I won't be like that. Even if my husband is a cobbler or a drunk, I won't..." She stopped herself as she looked to the pond's surface.

I raised myself up on my elbows and said plainly, "You don't have to marry, you know."

Lillian shook her head and said more softly, "Yes, I do Jo. My father..." She stopped herself again, then turned back to me, her usual cheer dulled.

"My father expects me to return home, during all breaks, after school, and for the rest of my life. He *wants* me--" Her voice broke. She closed her eyes and composed herself before continuing. "If I want to have a home of my own, I need to marry. Before school ends."

She looked back to the water and kicked a few pebbles in, disturbing the still water.

"You could earn a vocation? I am quite excited about the aspect of secretary school--"

"I can't. I won't...I've never done such a thing." She scoffed. "And if I fail, I would have to go back to him. I don't have your talent or your determination or your forgiving home, Jo."

I felt my nails dig brutally into the earth. She was always hesitant to talk about her father, but when she did, the hatred was loud. He introduced himself during the beginning of the school year. A rotund belly filled with excess and a red beard oiled to a sack shape. He'd looked down at me through tiny circled frames and asked in a booming voice if I wanted to visit during Christmas. Lillian had jumped in of course, saying I was taking a holiday elsewhere and would be unable to. He'd clicked his tongue against his teeth and said, "Pity."

"Luckily for you, there are plenty of toads in this water who would love a kiss. A prince is better than a cobbler by far."

That pulled a smile from Lily; she raised her pale linen skirt and placed a foot into the water.

"It's nearly tepid--"

"Lily, don't, you'll come out freezing with nothing to warm you or even to dry off. You're ill-prepared."

She looked over, and cocked her head. "So you won't join me?"

I shook my head sharply and raised myself to sit, sticking to my spot.

She shrugged and scrunched up her blouse, the intricate white lace crinkling, and asked over her shoulder, "Is anyone near?"

I looked behind us. I saw and heard nothing from the small cluster of trees that hid the back street. There was no one present but us around the pond.

"No one, but me."

"You don't count, you silly filly."

I twitched my nose. "What phrase is that? Did one of the other girls teach you that?"

She pulled her blouse off and threw it next to me. "Madeline Jameson quite enjoys rhymes. If she has a nimble of port, she's full of them."

"That sounds cruel...Do you mean it in jest?"

Lillian kicked over her skirt, turned in her cream chemise, and walked backwards into the pool, the water meeting at her ankle.

"I don't mean to be cruel. In all honesty, your company is the only one I can bear--"

She said something else, but my attention was captured by the sun peeking from the cloud and hitting her perfectly at the water's edge. If this sight was seen centuries ago in Greece, the viewer would be convinced that this subject was praised by Apollo himself. The gods have their favorites.

"Jo? Aren't you listening?"

She had sunk now waist deep, moving her arms through the water.

"Sorry?"

"I asked if the headmistress took the card?"

I exhaled a breath I didn't realize was being held. "Oh...No. She said it could only be kept if I appreciated it and its importance--"

"Importance?"

"She said someone had made them for divination. They were hand-painted so they must have been very special to whoever owned them."

"That's brilliant! So did you add it to our collection?"

I nodded and held my knees to my chest, rubbing my thumb nail.

"We must be careful from now on. I was given a warning about... our friendship. Martin's fearful we may get in the way of what we are to take away from the Hibbert School--"

"At least she was kind in her *suggestion*. Mrs. Dansfield told me that I was to avoid you at all costs. You know what I said?"

"What?"

"I told her I pitied her to not understand closeness. It was a dreadful thing to be so alone."

I gasped. "What on earth did she say to that?"

Lily winced and began getting out, the chemise sticking to her thin frame.

"She didn't find that words would get her message across, so she simply gave me a lashing on my arm. Oh, and said I am not allowed to go to the fete tomorrow. No sweet buns and hymns for me."

She walked out and kneeled on the grass, offering her forearm to me. I took it and saw across her olive skin a thin and long violet bruise.

"It doesn't hurt..." she said, watching my face turn and tremble at the sight.

"I'm sorry I got you into this."

"It was an effort on both our parts--"

"Luckily, you're leaving within the year. You won't have to be bothered by Mrs. Dansfield or..."

Tears began pouring from my eyes, dripping onto her arm. She tsked then reached out for me, pulling me into a tight hug.

She said in a quiet secretive voice, "I'll write every day and I'll visit, of course, I'll visit."

A bell rang out across the grounds, two loud hits.

Lily pulled away and grabbed her blouse and skirt. "Dinner is to start and I am looking as if I drowned."

"I could save you a seat or even some food if you don't come down in time?"

"That would save a headache. Thanks, Jo!" She rushed off, putting the blouse and skirt on quickly. All you could see from under the tree was the stretch of hill and the pointed tops of the dual spires made of scrubbed limestone that seemed to tetter every winter. I saw Lily reach the top of the hill, wave quickly, then disappear on the other side of the path.

I stood, briefly rubbing my own bare forearm.

***

The next day at noon, students were let out early to celebrate St. George's Day. All of us exited from our classes and calmly walked out of the main doors except for myself, who languished the whole affair. If I could just sneak off to Lillian's room, we could celebrate the day together and she wouldn't have to see it as such a punishment. I let the other girls skip in front of me and followed further behind, my shoes clicking on the front stone steps. Then I saw Lily at the side gate grinning ear to ear. My smile began and fell when I saw it was an older man, gripping the gate with one hand and leaning his head against it. He was absorbing every word she was saying feverishly. He nodded and smiled, charmed.

I walked up briskly behind her and asked, coldly, "Who's this?"

The man looked up with dark blue eyes and greasy brown hair. He grinned suddenly and asked in a thick Irish accent, "This her then?"

Lily nodded and pulled me closer, just a few inches from his face. "Jo, I was just telling him about our recent trouble-making."

I snapped my head over to her. "Why would you tell some stranger about that?"

Lily scoffed and was about to say something when the man interrupted her.

"Lets' fix that, shall I? Name is Marcus and I'm..."

She grabbed my arm and said happily, "He's a magician!"

Unimpressed, I pulled Lily back. "We should really go--"

"Just watch, Jo."

He smiled at Lily and produced a thick gold coin. He flicked it through his fingers, held it up and squeezed it in his palm, and opened it to show nothing.

"It's some parlour trick." I said, trying to move away once more, but the man moved his hand through the bars to point at me.

"Check yer hair."

I reached up behind my left ear and felt something thick in the frizz. I pulled out the coin from its position. I held it up, my heart racing. He stood there smugly and proud of my confusion.

"That's not even the real magic. I've done all sorts, the mundane, the maddening--It's good fun. You'd like it." He winked at me, sending a shiver down my spine.

He flicked his eyes to Lily, who returned with a moon-eyed stare. She looked positively foolish.

"Magic tricks only work on children," I said proudly, crossing my arms across my chest.

He grinned this terrible smile, all teeth with the corners of his mouth pulled back. I didn't want to unpack the wild look growing in his eye.

"Tricks yeah, but not real magic. Real magic isn't something to toy with." He rolled his tongue over his teeth.

Lillian pouted her lips, trying to mimic the picture of Sarah Bernhardt that she kept on her nightstand. "You can do that then?" she asked, cocking her head and leaning against the gate.

"Aye" was all he said, setting his head against the gate bar, parallel to her.

I pulled Lillian back and said, "Magic isn't real. Lillian. He is just trying to beg for money--"

She wriggled out of my grasp and stared at me with a raised eyebrow and sour expression. "Josephine, where on earth are your manners? I didn't realize you had the social graces of a Scottish goat."

I stepped back, clutching my chest, feeling as though a wound was forming.

Lillian gave an exasperated sigh and turned back to Marcus. "Forgive her, she...she is guarded."

He gave a long look, one strangely familiar. "She should be. It's a chaotic world out here; you never know who could sneak in."

Bastard. "And what are your intentions? We have no money and we aren't to leave school grounds, so I see no usefulness to you," I asked, folding my arms tightly under my chest.

He clicked his tongue and said, "Just because you don't see it, don't mean it isn't there."

"Get away from the gate!"

Lillian and I moved back and saw Mrs. Martins, picking up her skirts from the stairs and marching over. Her back was perfectly straight, giving her the air of utmost grace and reserve. She was a stunning maid. She had given her youth to protect and teach the girls who had entered our Hibbert School. The years were stolen from her, but they were not thankless.

"Girls, go to East Hall for the celebration."

Lillian piped up, "Ma'am, I'm not allowed. I was just helping Mr..."

I shot her an impatient look. Was she to defend him? To uphold his honor which he obviously lacked.

"Now. Your punishment will further be discussed later," Mrs. Martins said, without a tone of desperation or anger, but it was unmoving and it was to be followed.

We walked solemnly past the steps onto the uneven stone path that ran the length of the school. I paused at the side of the West Hall, looking past the washed white stone bricks and saw he was shaking her hand, amicable.

***

"You've heard then?"

I bit into the soft red apple then passed it to her, replying, "Heard what?"

She bit into it as well then said, "Apparently there is to be a show this Friday. Courtesy of that magician."

She held it out, but I didn't take it.

"Performing? How on earth did he manage that?"

She looked to me, eyebrows knitted together, letting her hand drop into her lap. "He is, and I, for one, am excited--He said he was going to perform a real trick before you spoiled it."

She tried to hide the disappointment in her voice. She offered the apple once more.

I crossed my arms and said, "You seemed quite entranced with him. I'm surprised he didn't perform it already."

She didn't respond to that.

I thought he was gone by now. The red came to my cheeks. I rubbed them angrily.

"He shouldn't be here. What are we to do with a show?"

"Do you not get bored here? It's so dreary. It makes me miss Munich."

I picked up a stick and began to mess with a small pile of rocks by the water's edge. "I thought you hated Munich."

She stuck her tongue to her molar and scoffed. "I hate living with my father. I miss living in civilization."

I set my chin on my left shoulder and asked, "I don't think anyone would accuse Northern England of being uncivilized."

She laughed, then pretended to cough into her hand.

"Stop it. I'm trying to be mad at you."

"Please don't be. You understand why I dislike him so much, surely?"

Lillian began picking at the tilted blades of grass. "Because he was focused on me and not you."

I huffed and said in soft desperation, "Of course not. It's because he is much older and--"

Lillian stood and put her hands on her hips. "He is not much older than most suitors."

"You've just turned seventeen..."

"We aren't children, Jo! We shouldn't be so lost in childish things. I was..." She stopped, her bottom lip trembling. "I was going to gift you a typewriter so you could write me once I leave. Now you've ruined it." She gathered up her skirts and walked under the polar's shade.

I stepped on the edge of the shadow and begged, "Nothing has to change. We don't have to change, not for any man or each other... I want you to be happy-"

"Exactly what I want, which is why I wish to marry someone fun."

"Fun? You may as well marry a carnival performer."

"Perhaps I will, and you'll be a maid and waste away like Mrs. Dansfield..." She had gone too far and knew it. My lip trembled a moment.

I turned on my heel and marched up the side of the grassy hill.

After walking onto the pavement between the hill and main hall, I heard a whistle. I wouldn't have given it a thought, but it felt direct, like a bird call. I turned and saw a man inside the gate, the Magician.

He shouldn't be here, not inside.

I began walking briskly through the main doors. My pace quickened feeling his eyes on my back.

How on earth did he get in?

***

She wasn't there. Mrs. Dansfield just paused over Lily's seat when taking attendance and never said a word about it. I kept staring at it as if she would appear suddenly, but her seat was bare and the gnawing of her pencil absent. After class concluded, I walked with slow and careless steps so I could spot her coming around some sharp corner or pausing in a doorway, but nothing. I thought I saw the bouncing of her braid, but it was gone when I blinked. While sitting in Practical Sewing, I thought I heard the clacking of her favorite Parisian shoes, but I couldn't be sure. While threading my needle through the end of a pillow sack that looked more like a hood, I thought, *she'll be at the lake waiting for me, I know it.* I stabbed my thumb when thinking of what she would say.

Class ended promptly at 11:30, which left me 10 minutes to rush down before lunch began. I grabbed a handful of my skirt and ran out of the school with my writing books pinned to my side with my right arm. I made it to the top of the hill and shielded my eyes from the sun. A figure sat beneath our tree, but it was impossible to make out. I rushed down the hill, collecting grass stains at the end of my skirt and skidding on the wet grass fresh with dew. I was a few yards away when I saw painfully clearly it wasn't Lily.

It was Marcus lounging against the tree. He had one knee to his chest and leaned an arm on it with a wide-brimmed hat hiding his face. He looked like a ridiculous version of the men I grew up around, drunk miners napping on their break. I stepped carefully toward him, dropping my skirt, stepping on it carelessly. When I made it to the shadow of the tree, he raised his head, finally showing his red-streaked cheeks and an apple in his mouth. He pulled it out, a clear-cut impression of his teeth in its flesh.

"You made it."

My mouth dropped then raised, my chin sticking out proudly. "Lily..."

He shrugged, throwing the apple up in the air and then catching it. "She stepped out. Went to the kitchen to grab me a bite."

"She...Sshe's feeding you now?" I...I didn't mean to ask that. I didn't.

He offered the apple to me which I didn't even humor. "Your school is giving me a good 'mount of money, but not till after the show. Luckily, I have kindness to rely on."

I felt the bile rise up in my mouth. I had to turn my head away. "How can she not see it..." I whispered it under my breath, a thought that kept running through my mind and sticking to each side.

He leaned his head against the tree, the hat brim folding in. He was watching me again in that strange familiar way that touched me since the first day he arrived.

"Money..." I said suddenly, stepping in the shade of the tree. "That's what you want, right?"

He didn't respond, just raised an eyebrow.

"I can give you money. More than the school and I'd give it..."

"You couldn't..." he said, his eyes narrowing.

"I have it. In jewelry and cloth, and, and..." My mind escaped me and I said curtly, "I will give you anything just to leave us alone."

"Us, eh?"

"You..." I bit my tongue, hard.

He leaned forward, staring up at me in some mock hopelessness. "You...You what? Should I not say her name? Should I test out what happens if I do?"

I dug my heels into the dirt, my face turned deep red and a vein popping in the center of my forehead.

"Don't." It was all I could manage to say.

He got on his knees, and looked up at me like a parishioner begging for confession in church.

"Lillian."

It sounded like a pop of a shooting rifle. The noise blanketed what I did next. I screamed, a hollow shrill scream that tightened my chest. He didn't look frightened, he looked more intrigued. That made the world blur around me. I grabbed ahold of his shirt and began ripping at the cloth, handfuls, and just pulled. The threads snapped and the right sleeve came off in my hand. He still didn't stop me, just looked at me more disappointed. I reached for the red scarf around his neck and pulled, jerking his head forward like strangling a doll.

Then he put his hands over my wrists and held them. I stopped, feeling the touch awfully chilly and almost seeping into my skin.

"Josephine, it doesn't have to be like this," he said, the grip softening.

I dropped my hands, frightful suddenly of the feeling sunk deep through my fine hairs and freckles.

The bell rang loud over the property, causing a family of birds to rise from the trees and fly across the sky.

He sighed, picked himself up, and straightened his scarf. As he was straightening it further he said, "This is what's gonna happen. You are going to stand by, wishing me dead while I get my way. It'll happen now and it'll happen over and over again." He put his hand to his chest and sighed. "I'm sorry."

He walked away, past the trees and onto the handmade path back onto the main road. Frozen at the pond, I pressed my own hand to my chest, feeling the sickening quick beat of my heart.

***

The banner above the East Hall's front door announced "Marcus Magnus Presents." Danielle and Mary Vaughn were failing to put up the accompanying poster inside the foyer due to an argument of the placement. I made my way swiftly under the banner into the theater. Other girls were milling about, setting up the rest of the chairs and helping Madame Dupuy set up a large bowl of lemonade and cookies the size of compasses and just as tasteless. I looked around the room for Lillian who surely would have arrived sooner. It had been over a day since seeing her and I was fearful I would have forgotten her face.

Finally I saw her exiting the side of the dusty red curtain with a happy but nervous expression. She was pressing her thumb between her front of her teeth, a tell-tale sign she was planning on doing something devious. I had seen the expression before, many times.

She skipped down the stage steps and went over to Madame Dupuy to help. Then she saw me. She looked like she was about to say something aloud, but she closed her mouth and turned back to Dupuy with a more solemn expression.

What had he done to her? I stepped toward her unconsciously, but doubled back. I was only here to do one thing.

***

He stared at himself in the mirror of the dressing room. He turned his head to see the vein thick on his neck and the dull shadow of a beginning beard. Carefully I entered, then his eye turned on me in the mirror's reflection.

"You're late," he said, making direct eye contact.

"I--I--" All my bravery had left me. I could feel what I wanted to say, the screams and thrashing, but it added to nothing. Nothing I did would reveal any truth to Lily. Nothing...

Marcus broke into my thoughts. "No speech? No declarations? I'm disappointed." He stood and dropped something into a small dish with a metal clank.

My lip quivered and I croaked, "Go. Please." My voice barely sounded like my own.

He hooked a hand into his neck scarf and grinned menacingly.

"I know what you are..." he began, his Irish accent prominent.

My tongue rattled in my mouth, too angry to say anything.

"You are lying to yourself." He looked away from the mirror and took a step toward me.

I stepped back. "I am not."

"Indeed ya are." One more step.

"You, sir, know nothing of me--"

"I know you, and Miss Lillian, and with that, I know a great deal."

I stepped back, blood pumping into my clenched fists.

"I'm not afraid of you."

He held out of his hands. "Aye, not of me, but you are tongue-tied and scared. I'm not allowed to say of what."

He advanced forward methodically. I stepped backwards, stepping on sheets of strewn paper and cracked beads from old costumes.

"I am not...I am..." My voice quivered saying it, the anger slipping.

"Ya are." He was close now, I could see the unevenly-stitched spades in his waistcoat.

"I don't like this."

He nodded, licking his lips. "Good."

I stepped into the wall, pressing my palms against the striped wallpaper. He stopped in front of me, the smell of old paper rich on his skin.

"What do you want from me?" I said it through shaking lips. He knelt to look me in the eye, his green-fleckedbrown eyes nearly matching my own.

"I want you to say it."

"Say--?"

He slammed his hand above my head.

"She's taken to me. Lillian, darling thing, she said she likes me dress and me charm and me ability...She asked to meet me late tonight...by the pond."

My eye twitched, I grabbed him by his waistcoat and jerked him to me. "Don't speak of her or to her. Erase her from your mind."

He tsked, "If only I could. I've taken a fancy to her."

I pushed him back hard, his foot tripping over the other. He steadied himself.

"I like her, love her even. How her hair moved in the breeze, how the silk collected to her legs when she walked out of the pond--" His voice drifted off as my head found the image. It was the day before we had met him.

"You...you were watching us? How..."

The anger flooded my mind, but something was sticking.

"No...We were alone. It was just us then..."

He dropped his smile and nodded.

"Say it."

I opened my mouth, then closed it.

He stuffed his hands in his pockets and waited.

I looked wildly as if the answer was floating between us. Lillian and I were alone then I was sure of it, but my attention did drift. I was watching her and unwilling to get into the pond myself. I swore she looked--

He interrupted my thoughts, "She looked divine as if she worshipped some sun god."

My eyes grew wide.

He looked like he understood. "You must say the truth, Josephine. Say what you have been unable to say. I can't say it for you."

"I...." I felt it in my chest, like the words were ironclad and sunk to the bottom. "I can't...She'll never understand."

He shook his head. "No matter."

My hands shook, going to my mouth, the shock sinking in. "I think I...."

He exhaled a deep breath and closed his eyes.

I moved my hands to my chest and moved them over my heart.

"I love her...I love Lily."

I blinked quickly and he was gone. The room was still except the nearby sound of chairs scraping against the floor in the theatre. My breath quivered and the lump in my throat dropped away. Where Marcus stood was something fam-liar. I walked over and picked it up. In my hands was Le Batelevr.

***

"Josephine, you must tell what Miss Albrecht's involvement was? Did she tell you to take it?" the headmistress asked sternly.

I wrung my hands, boring holes into them. Meekly I said, "She did no such thing. I...I took it in fear it would be discarded or unappreciated."

"To what end, dear? This could very well be the beginning to a life of vice..."

I looked up quickly and scooted forward in the chair.

"If that may be, it is from not accepting consequences of my own actions. Lillian had nothing to do with it. Lily is...She's...Well, she deserves much more than I."

Ms. Martin let out a heavy sigh, then picked up the card and tapped it on the table. "You are much too hard on yourself."

"It's not that. It's just...If I could, I would give her goodness... I don't mean in character, I mean in security and comfort. She wants to marry and shed her goodness only to honor some man who knows nothing of her--" I stopped, seeing Ms. Martin's expression softened, and she gripped the card more tightly.

"Mrs. Martin?"

"I understand, Josephine...I developed very close relationships when I was your age as well. I understand completely. I also see you will adjust your ways accordingly to not steal or collect more treasures that were not bought by your own hand, understood?"

I nodded fiercely.

She offered the card to me, which I accepted.

"See to it that you treasure that card. It's a very unique item."

"How so, Mrs. Martin?"

"It's a divination card. My aunt was a fond collector for peculiar things. She showed me one very similar when I was younger than you. They are used to uncover truths, whether it be the future or the present. I believe this card, when pulled, means it is now the time to manifest your true desire,s or how my aunt put it, all you need to do is say what you want and the Almighty will grant it...But my aunt was quite fanciful," she said with a small smile.

I looked at it lovingly. "Do you think it can?"

She pulled her glasses off and folded them. "I think cards like that are simply a medium that we cast our own wants and desires onto and only interpret them how we want. If you were to pull it, you would read it in a way that interprets your own wants and desires. I do hope you cherish it. You will put it somewhere safe, yes?"

I put the card to my chest and said, "Yes, I will."

Chokeleaf

M.J. Garland

M.J. Garland was born and raised in
Fairbanks, Alaska and lives in Eastern
Massachusetts, where she works in
affordable housing development.

On our first night in the park, we sit around the campfire and take turns screaming into a ficus.

Devin presses the ball of leaves to his lips, and his face goes red with effort. He moves it away for a moment and I can hear him belt out a B-flat. When he brings the leaves back to his lips, the noise vanishes. He moves them back and forth, the sound disappearing and reappearing like a coin in a magician's palm.

When he's done, he lets the leaves rest in his lap. He looks pleased, and also a little freaked out.

"That's uncanny." His voice is raspier now and weaker, like the leaves clawed it out of him. A mosquito lands on his sweaty forehead, but he doesn't seem to notice.

"Is it your first time seeing *Ficus effusio*?" Mark asks. He's our Trail Captain, in his mid-twenties maybe, with condescension in his voice that even the densest cluster of leaves couldn't absorb.

"That's the scientific name for Chokeleaf?" Devin smiles, and it's apparent to me from the discolored patches on his teeth that he had braces until recently.

"Yes. *Ficus effusio*." Mark says it like it's a magic spell. Devin peers at the leaves in his lap again. "I haven't."

Kennedy reaches for the ball of leaves, the glow of the campfire reflected in her clear nail polish. "Me neither. May I try?"

I don't say anything. Last year, I had Chokeleaf plants in pots in each of the four corners of my dorm room, because my roommate Celia liked country music and no one else on our floor could tolerate it at any volume. With the Chokeleaf there to absorb the sound, we could blast whatever music we wanted and no RA's came to our door to remind us that We Live in a Community.

"You got spit all over it." Kennedy curls her lip in mock-disgust, but holds the plant to her mouth anyway. She takes a big breath in through her nose and then I can tell she is singing or screaming or yelling, because the smooth skin on her cheeks crease, and folds take shape on either side of her face that flank her mouth like parentheses. When she pulls the leaves away from her lips, the sound is so loud my whole body tenses. As soon as she hears her own yell, she presses the plant to her lips again, but even the half-second of noise is like a hand clapped over my eardrum.

Rishi tries next. He tucks his longish wavy hair behind his ears, then holds the leaves to his lips and strains like the singer in a metal band. I can picture him onstage, electric guitars shrieking behind him. When he's done, he passes the ball to me, then uses the hem of his T-shirt to wipe the sweat from his face. I try to compress the circular leaves, but they are already so dense I can barely make the lump smaller. I press it to my mouth and scream as loudly as I can until my lungs ache. The plant swallows the sound.

The others start talking before I am finished screaming.

"Why did you kids join Trailblazers?" Mark asks. It's a question purportedly for all of us, but his eyes are fixed on Kennedy.

"I'm on a gap year, and I've always been passionate about eradicating invasive species." Kennedy gives the sort of self-satisfied smile that would fit in well at the end of a job interview or campaign speech. "What about everyone else?"

I continue to scream into the leaves, though my lungs ache. I can feel a pressure in my ears from the screaming, but I can still hear everything that's going on around me. It *is* uncanny, to scream without hearing my own scream. When I'm out of breath, I rest the lump of plant matter in my lap. Mosquitoes swarm me, despite the smoke. I watch one land on my arm and I jerk, trying to get it to fly away so I don't have to swat it.

Rishi plays with the hem of his T-shirt, a faded one emblazoned with the name of some band I'm not cool enough to know about. "I just like being in nature, so I thought 'hell yeah, I'll get paid to camp.'"

Devin nods. "Same. I want to learn survival skills, so that I can outlive the impending collapse of this society."

Mark snorts at that.

"What about you, Steph?" Rishi turns towards me, firelight reflected in his irises.

"I'm taking a break from school," I say, which is sort of the truth. I'm on involuntary medical leave, my university's way of saying *If you're going to kill yourself, please do it off-campus.*

Mark shakes his head. "You'll find that Trailblazers is no break. This is demanding work, physically and mentally. But it's also rewarding."

I give him a weak smile, then stare out into the forest rather than make any more eye contact. I can see at least six Chokeleaf shrubs from my seated position, all about as tall as me, their thin branches dripping with leaves so small and densely packed they form a dark green wall. I'm used to seeing Chokeleaf in pots. Seeing them in the wild feels different; uncontained, they remind me that I'm in their home, they're not in mine.

"Let's roast marshmallows!" Devin springs up from his seated position and rummages through our bear canister of dry goods. When he circles the fire, handing us each a marshmallow and a Chokeleaf branch, I accept both.

I strip the leaves off the branch and impale my marshmallow, then hold the stick so it hovers an inch above the coals. I do not feel like I am camping yet. I feel like I am acting out "camping", like it's a word I've drawn in Charades.

The other Trailblazers look like they are acting out camping, too, but they are more committed to their roles. Rishi is whittling the tip of his stick with a pocketknife. Devin is poking at the fire, like he's afraid it'll fall asleep. Mark slaps his own cheek with one hand, leaving the smear of a dead mosquito in his brown stubble, now auburn with blood. Firelight glimmers off a stray wing, turning it iridescent.

When I was little, maybe eight or nine, I found a dragonfly floating on top of a puddle outside of my house. I lifted it out of the water, marveling at how light it felt in my hand, and rested it in the grass. It moved enough that I could tell it was alive, but it could not fly with its waterlogged wings. I was worried something would come and eat it while it was helpless, so I watched it for what felt like hours as its wings dried in the sun, their intricate pattern of lines and circles glowing purple and green in the late afternoon light. At last, it flew away, just as my parents called me for dinner. I went inside and ate a hamburger, but about halfway through I started to feel the texture of its fat and muscle in my mouth, reminding me it had once walked around. My mother insisted I could not go to my room without finishing my dinner, so I sat at the table with half a burger in front of me until nightfall, when I gave up and ate it because I was hungry anyway.

There's a sour taste in my mouth as I think about the dragonfly, a taste I know won't be drowned out by a s'more. Devin stops messing with the fire for a momentand gets up to go inside his tent. When he returns, he has a ukulele in one hand. My mood worsens, something I hadn't thought possible. He sits down and starts strumming and singing that John Denver song about country roads. His voice is undeniably good, but I still keep an eye on the woods behind his back, secretly hoping that the country roads will show up to take him home.

I realize too late that my marshmallow is charred, the sugary outside burnt black. I eat it anyway, first pulling off the crunchy outside and letting it fall to ash in my mouth.

Mark stands up and moves around the campfire. His hair is shorter on the sides, so he looks like a crested bird. He bobs like a bird, too, when he walks. He takes a seat by Kennedy and leans over to talk to her. I can hear enough snippets to tell it's a hiking story, something about a time he was close to a bear.

I am consumed suddenly and utterly by the urge to not be here, though I also do not want to be at my parents' house. I am homesick for last year's dorm, but now a stranger lives on my side of the room and Celia is living somewhere else with someone else. I pick up the Chokeleaf wreath and press it to my lips again. I scream and scream until it's time to go to sleep.

***

Seven hours drain away on a leaking inflatable sleeping pad and then I wake with my back indented from pebbles. At breakfast, Mark lectures us over mugs of instant coffee.

"*Ficus effusio*, or Chokeleaf as you know it by its common name, is a man-made abomination, engineered in a lab to absorb all but the lowest frequencies of sound. Since its accidental introduction to Wild Canyon Park, Chokeleaf has caused animal populations to shrink as creatures can no longer find one another to mate." He shakes the ball of leaves in his hand. "This invasive species is claiming human lives along with animal ones; multiple hikers have disappeared after becoming separated from their friends. We are here for the next eight weeks to take our park back."

I haven't changed my base layer from yesterday and everything feels slightly damp, but the upside is that I haven't had to look at my body in days. The smoke from yesterday's campfire lingers in my hair, so I smell like a burned witch. I check my phone, but there's no signal. No text messages have made their way through, or perhaps no one has texted me.

Across the campfire from me, Kennedy pours coffee into her mug of oatmeal and mixes the two with a spork. I look down at my own mug, which contains a similar mixture. The nice thing about camping is that everyone else eats like they've given up, too.

Mark is in his element, gesticulating away. "The only positive quality of *Ficus effusio* is that the trunks are so slender you can easily sever them with just a pair of shears. So, don't worry; none of you will have to handle a heavy axe or a scary chainsaw."

Kennedy and I make eye contact and I see her suck in her lower lip as she struggles not to laugh.

"If you do encounter a trunk too thick for the shears, find me and I'll use my axe." Mark pats the axe which leans against his foot.

"Your goal is to chop down as many *Ficus effusio* as possible, while leaving the other plants untouched. If you get separated from your partner, don't bother yelling for one another. Just let off one of your flares. The same goes if you can't find the camp-ground. Now, finish your breakfast and get partnered up. And remember to leave no trace. I don't want to find a trail of candy wrappers in the woods."

Kennedy makes eye contact again, and for a moment I don't know why. Then, I realize she wants to be my partner.

I scrape the last of my oatmeal into the fire and head over to her. She looks absurdly put together considering our surroundings, like the kind of daughter my parents would have wanted to have. Her dark hair is in a neat ponytail and she's wearing a cream-colored North Face fleece jacket under her Trailblazers wind-breaker that somehow has escaped any traces of dirt.

"Hey," she says, "How'd you sleep?"

"Good." I haven't had a reason to speak today, and when I do I can feel the soreness in my throat from last night's screaming.

"That's good for you," she says, her voice bright. "I barely slept. It's so cold at night here."

She looks alert to me, though there is a trace of a shadow under each of her brown eyes. I'm marveling at the fact that I'm even out of my tent. At the beginning of my medical leave, I left my single psychiatrist's appointment with a prescription for Wellbutrin, and it's helped with my energy level if nothing else.

Kennedy and I carve a slow path through the woods, stopping to cut down Chokeleaf as we go. The leaves of the trees we cut down are full of water, so our damp clothes grow even colder and wetter as we progress. The forest is so devoid of sound that

I become uncomfortably aware of the noises I am making just digesting and breathing. My stomach rumbles like I have an ice-maker inside me.

Kennedy talks constantly as we walk, telling me about her family at home and the college she's going to next year and her five-year plan.

"It's just nice being here and getting space to breathe," Kennedy says. "I like my brothers and sister, but it's good to finally have some privacy."

I nod, even though a campsite isn't my idea of privacy.

I spot another cluster of Chokeleaf plants and use my shears to sever the slender trunks at their base. I tuck a bundle of the leaves into my pocket.

"Souvenir?" Kennedy asks.

"Handkerchief."

"So you can sneeze silently?"

"Yeah. And if Mark says something stupid, I can hide my laugh."

She grins, exposing a row of straight, white teeth. "That's brilliant."

I don't reply. My palms are already sore from the shears, and I just want to be back in bed.

"Look at that." Kennedy points and I turn my gaze.

There's a bird hopping around on the branch of a nearby Chokeleaf tree. It flaps its wings in an exaggerated dance, opening its beak in silent squawks.

Kennedy claps a hand over her mouth to hide her giggle. "It looks so funny."

I feel suddenly very distant from her, as if we are on opposite ends of the woods with no chance of us ever seeing or hearing each other. I stand there and watch the bird calling for a mate as the forest eats its song.

**

The days take on a pattern. I go to bed stiff from the cold and wake up even stiffer. In the morning, I take my meds, then stuff a sock into the bottle so it won't rattle in my backpack. I check my phone, but there's never any signal and even if there was, I can't imagine anyone would message me. I open Instagram and stare at the blank white squares, images that haven't loaded. Then, I join the others outside the tent. We gather around the fire and eat oatmeal, which never tasted like much to me and now tastes like even less. I never have to talk much, because the others seem intent on speaking incessantly. In the few breaks in the conversation, the silence surprises me in its immensity.

On a foggy morning in our third week in the park, Kennedy and I walk into the woods together. The silence presses down on us. It feels equal parts suffocating and comforting, like a weighted blanket.

A strand of hair has escaped from Kennedy's ponytail and she brushes it out of her face. "I'm so sick of sleeping outside. I don't know why people do this for fun."

I nod. I think people like camping because the novelty of being miserable all the time is interesting to them. It's not for people like me, who are already miserable.

Kennedy continues to talk. "At least it's not as bad here as being at home."

I nod again, even though I'm not sure I agree.

Apparently, I don't need to say anything to keep the conversation going, because she keeps talking. "I can't wait until college."

She stares off into the distance, as if she's looking at a bright future and not endless trees.

I keep my eyes on the underbrush. "College is better than high school, definitely."

She uses her shears to chop down a Chokeleaf plant. "So, you like it?"

"I liked parts." I squat down in order to sever a trunk at the base, already regretting participating in this conversation.

"Which parts?"

I'm starting to feel like I'm being cross-examined, but when I glance up at her she's still smiling. Leaves overhead cast a shadow pattern across part of her face so she looks like she's wearing a lacy mask.

"I had some really good friends," I say, thinking of Celia. I had other friends, of course, but they forgot about me sooner. I didn't answer their texts my last semester, didn't show up to our shared classes, and pretty soon they weren't trying to reach out anymore.

Kennedy turns away from me, so she sounds much quieter, none of her soundwaves bouncing back to me from the forest. "If you like college, then why are you taking time off?"

I feel something solid in my gut. "Because I was having a hard time."

"Oh." She is silent for a moment. "That's pretty mature, to realize that something is wrong and do something about it."

"It wasn't my decision," I say. "My school told me I needed to take time off until I was better."

"And you don't agree?"

I look down at my feet. "I think it was easier for me to handle things at school."

She turns back to me. "Why? I mean, isn't college stressful?"

College hadn't been perfect, but it was better than my childhood house, a dimly lit and silent place. My mother had awful migraines, so intense that at times she hallucinated a bright light like the headlight of a train barreling towards her. In the throes of a migraine, she would lock herself in her dark bedroom and insist that no one make a sound. After she had recovered from a migraine and stepped back into the rest of the house, she would frown if she saw anything out of place, like the crust of a sandwich on my plate or a toy in front of the sofa. When she went to lie down and nurse her migraine, I would tiptoe around the house, cleaning up my messes. I felt like a spy, trying to sweep away my tracks as I moved through the house, trying always to look like I had never been there. Even when she was fine, I treaded carefully, searching for the signs in her brow and gaze that she was on the edge of developing a migraine. Each small noise I made, from joy or sorrow, could cause her pain. Even speaking was scary to me; my voice could easily be too loud, or there could be an unintentional impolite meaning to my words that would cause my mother to turn away and pretend I did not exist. It had been liberating to move in with Celia and share a room with someone who wanted me to exist, and sometimes even to exist loudly.

Kennedy's voice jolts me out of my thoughts. "Why were things easier to handle at school?"

"My roommate was always there for me." I think about Celia, how she would sneak orzo salad and bananas out of the cafeteria for me when I didn't have the energy to get out of bed.

"She sounds like a good friend."

My eyes tear up at the thought of Celia, and how I've disappeared from her life completely. "She is."

"Is everything okay?"

"Yes." I regret saying so much. I stare at my grimy hands.

Kennedy is quiet for a moment, and I realize just how silent the pocket of forest is where we are standing. I can hear my pulse hammering, so loudly I'm worried Kennedy can hear it, too.

Her brown eyes are full of sympathy. "I'm sure she misses you a lot, too."

I force a smile. "Maybe we'll get back out of the woods and I'll have a million text messages from her."

She nods again. "That's probably right."

The idea makes me feel a little better, though I doubt it. I didn't respond to any of Celia's messages in the weeks after I moved out of the dorm and before I started Trailblazers. I'm not even sure why; I just knew it would ache to talk about any of it, about what we had—if we had anything—and about my life now.

I look around for more Chokeleaf to chop down. There's a cluster just a few feet away from me, but the trunks are far thicker than any I've seen before. Some are as thick as my torso.

"Look," I tell Kennedy.

She follows my gaze. "Those are giant."

I step forward without thinking, walking right into the center of the grove. I thought the rest of the forest was silent, but surrounded entirely by the trees, I now understand what true silence is. I close my eyes and watch red shapes swim across the insides of my eyelids as I listen to nothing, true nothing. The quiet is such that my brain attempts to fill it in. I can hear things that aren't real now; a distant ringing, a slight murmur, almost a song, like the ones Celia would play in our dorm.

Celia's cheeks were red and wisps of her hair floated as we danced around the room to *Follow Your Arrow*. Her body had a sixth sense—she could dance without running into the dressers or wardrobes or hampers or beds that crowded our tiny room. She grabbed my arm and spun me in a circle, then dipped me. I shrieked with laughter, not worried about anyone outside hearing us. She sang along, *Make lots of noise, kiss lots of boys, or kiss lots of girls if that's what you're into*. She pressed her lips against mine and I was breathless. When she broke away, I let out a whoop, knowing the Chokeleaf would swallow it. The Chokeleaf plants kept our joy contained, where it could be just for us, none of it leaking out of the room where it could be mocked or resented. There is no joy with me now, in this grove, but there is peace and a silence so deep it conjures the memory of music.

There was music playing a week after the kiss, when I finally opened up to Celia about how empty I'd felt the past six years. *I feel like I would be doing the world a favor if I just disappeared,*

I told her as we both sat cross-legged on her lofted bed, illuminated by the strings of lights that zig-zagged across the wall. She squeezed my arm. *I'll dial the number for Psychiatric Services,* she told me. *And when they pick up, I want you to ask for an appointment.* She dialed the number, then placed the phone on the comforter between us and we sat there, listening to it ring.

I jump when I feel the touch. I turn and see that Kennedy has extended her hand into the grove to grab my shoulder. She motions for me to come towards her.

I pull myself away and step out of the grove.

A tiny furrow appears between her brows. "I yelled and yelled, and you just stood there."

Her voice sounds loud to me now. I can't tell if this is because she's annoyed at me, or because I became used to the absolute silence of the grove.

"I'm sorry," I say. "It was just so peaceful."

She stares at me, her strong jaw set and her lips a straight line.

"They're too large for us to chop down," she says. "Mark can come get them tomorrow, with his axe."

I look back at the trees, standing so resolutely in their cluster, and think of them lying on the ground, leaking sap.

***

We gather around the campfire that night and make dinner, chopping peppers, potatoes, and sausages and wrapping them in foil before nestling the packets into the coals.

"I never thought I'd miss microwaves this much," Rishi says as he flips his foil packet with a stick. The stick pokes a hole in his foil packet and a hunk of potato falls out into the fire.

"Better get used to living without one." Devin grins, showing the ghosts of his braces again. "It's just not sustainable for Americans to keep living the way we've been living. We need to return to the basics, or else face inevitable collapse."

Rishi arches a brow, though the rest of his expression remains neutral. "That's not true. We have enough resources for everyone to have a good life, if we just distributed them better."

Kennedy cuts in. "I think what Devin's saying is not that we don't have enough to go around, but that the methods of producing these products aren't environmentally sustainable."

I tune them out, focusing instead on fishing my packet of food out of the fire. Using two sticks instead of Rishi's one, and holding them like tongs, proves effective. I open the packet and place a potato chunk in my mouth, but it's burning hot like a coal and I spit it back. I glance around, but no one is paying attention to me. I tune into and then out of the conversation. Mark is talking now, about how kids these days are so self-righteous it bores him to death. Kennedy objects and they bicker like siblings. I don't know where they get the energy for all this arguing, when it's wearing me out to just listen. I am unnecessary to this gathering, and everyone seems to have forgotten I'm here. I feel myself fading into the background, like the accumulated dirt on my skin has camouflaged me. I get up from the campfire, and no one glances at me.

"They're letting girls be Cub Scouts now!" Mark says to Kennedy as I walk away from the fire. "It's not fair to—"

His voice is cut off mid-sentence as I step into the forest, like I've slammed a door in his face. The silence is less menacing now that I'm on my own. It's almost relaxing, how it amplifies my breathing to the point where I cannot ignore it. I walk through the forest. The light is fading, and the world feels manageable, sound and sun held at bay. Maybe the reason the others talk so much is because they're afraid of this silence. For me at this moment, it feels like a respite. I walk until I find the grove, the cluster of thick Chokeleaf trees dark against the landscape.

I step into the center of the grove. The scent of my body, musty and rank, fills the tiny space in the center of the ring of trees. I can hear the saliva traveling down my throat when I swallow and my blood travelling through my body. I can hear everything in this tiny enclosure and nothing outside. The hush feels anticipatory, like the trees are waiting on me to speak or scream or sing, to feed them with my noise.

I feel like I am in a portal, like I am between places. For a moment, I just let myself exist in the silence. Then, I lie down in the center of the grove, a space just large enough to contain my body. I am completely alone in the dark, not even a bird song or the rustle of the wind to keep me company. A leaf falls onto my face and I rub it between my fingers, feeling the tiny ridges shaped like triangular prisms. I lie there in silence and watch the last traces of light drain from the sky. There is little difference in the darkness when my eyes are open versus shut, but I keep them open. I wonder why there aren't more stars, as far from the city as we are. I'd always wanted to see stars as a kid, to see any sort of nature beyond backyard insects, but we were too close to the city. I would have loved Trailblazers as a child, but now I don't like anything that requires effort. I wouldn't have even called my campus psychiatric services if Celia hadn't dialed the number for me.

I only ever had one appointment, with a therapist who seemed more on edge than I did. She wore a light-blue cardigan and her hair was up in a tight auburn bun. The art in her office was nondescript, landscapes in calming colors. I wondered if this was even her office and her art, or whether it was decorated by the school and shared by multiple therapists. I tried to imagine myself opening up to this woman, and reminded myself of what Celia had told me. *Take it one step at a time. The first step is showing up.* I was out of bed thanks to three alarms and an assist from Celia, but I didn't have the energy to give any expression other than neutral. She smiled at me, nervous energy sparking off her very white teeth, as she launched into a robotic intro.

"There are just a few questions I need to ask before we begin. In the past few weeks, have you wished you were dead?"

Without thinking, I nodded.

"Have you been having thoughts of killing yourself?"

I nodded again, even though I didn't really think of killing myself. I just thought of myself already dead, lying in the woods somewhere with moss reclaiming my body. The thought was peaceful to me.

I failed the suicide prevention screening, or passed it, maybe, depending on how you frame it. The therapist told my school I had a plan to kill myself, so I was placed on medical leave. The administrators say medical leave isn't a punishment, but it's the same thing they do to people who've broken the rules: make them leave campus for a while.

I didn't speak to Celia at all as I packed up my side of the dorm room. Tears and snot ran down her face as she told me again that she hadn't thought I was going to be kicked out. I didn't look at her. I wasn't angry, exactly, just numb, and seeing her face sent a stabbing pain through my heart.

I wish I could hear her voice now. I'm alone with the Chokeleaf, and the thought should make me feel sad, but instead I feel something else, or maybe what I'm feeling is nothing at all. I stare up at the dark green leaves above me, knowing that I could sing or scream or yell. The knowledge of all the possibilities makes me want to do nothing at all. I remain there, cradled in silence, as my breathing slows and a sense of deep calm washes over me.

***

I awaken to water dripping on my face and I open my eyes to the dense canopy above me, which is not quite dense enough to keep raindrops from hitting my face. For a moment, I struggle to remember where I am and how I got here. A wave of panic washes over me as I realize I have no idea how long I've been gone from camp. My blood pounds through my veins, thrumming loudly like the soundtrack to a horror film. I dig my fingers into my arm. *You idiot*, I think, as I realize how stupid it was to fall asleep among the trees. If anyone noticed I was gone and called for me, there was no way I could have heard them. They could have walked right by me, a foot from my head, and I would not have known. The thought makes my stomach twist.

I get to my feet and run out of the thicket. Outside of the grove, the wind whips my face. Rain is coming down hard, in diagonal sheets. I squint against the water blown into my face. The storm blows raindrops into my eyes like I'm crying in reverse. I run in the direction of the campsite, the world appearing before me in momentary flashes before my vision is again flooded. Twigs and brambles scratch at my ankles. The terrain is uneven and marred with branches and roots. I crash through clusters of trees, trip, right myself, and trip again.

Dread rises in me as I realize I've been running for too long. I should be at the campsite by now, but I'm not. I don't know where I am. I swing around and attempt to retrace my steps, blinking raindrops from my eyes as I scan the undergrowth. The Trailblazers could be calling for me, and I would still be unable to hear them. The idea is almost as horrifying as the more likely one, that they're not looking for me at all. The rain soaks through my windbreaker, which traps the water against my skin.

I stumble through the woods, none of it familiar. My boots are full of water and I'm shaking now, from the cold and from my fear. At last, I reach a copse of Chokeleaf. They're not as large as the ones in the grove where I slept, but their thick leaves provide some shelter from the rain. I step inside the thicket and the sound of the storm vanishes. I'm alone with my thoughts again and all I can think about is the others, the warmth of the campfire and the sound of their voices as they argue and complain and joke and bond. I'm tired of being alone. When I see another person, I want to sing and scream and talk until they have to acknowledge me, until we are forced to hear one another.

***

When I open my eyes, it's too bright sunlight, barely diluted by the canopy overhead. I'm confused for a moment about where I am. Then, I remember the previous night, the grove and the storm and my struggle to find shelter. The sun is directly above me, and harsh enough that I feel dizzy. It's day, perhaps even midday. My body is damp from the rain, and now I'm sweating, too, as I think about the others.

I get up and look around, hoping that in the light of day I'll be able to recognize my surroundings. I don't, and I've left multiple trails from crashing through the undergrowth the night before. I pick a direction and walk in it, hoping I'll see something familiar. My wet clothes chafe against my armpits, and my boots smell like someone died in them. I glance back and forth as I walk, searching for some clue to where the campsite might be. Everything is both familiar and not; each cluster of Chokeleaf looks like the last.

The sun sinks in the sky as I wander. My stomach aches from hunger, but my fear pushes me forward and I walk endlessly, hoping that over the next hill I will find the camp and its warm pocket of noise.

I continue walking into the evening, as the sky shifts to pink and then a deep blue. When I end up back at the same stand of trees where I slept the night before, I sink to a crouch and rock back and forth. I hug myself tightly and feel a cylindrical shape in my pocket.

The flare, I remember with a jolt. I pull it out. Matches are in an interior pocket of my jacket, where they've thankfully remained dry.

I strike the match and hold it to the flare. The flare must have gotten wet, because it doesn't light. I smell smoke, a wet, burnt smell, but the flare does not go off.

I strike another match and hold it to the flare. This time, the flame takes. As I watch the light arc across the sky, I wonder who will come to get me, if anyone comes at all. All I know is that I won't be able to hear them coming until they're already here.

Other Lives

Elizabeth Guilt

Elizabeth Guilt reads and writes short stories to make her daily commute on the London Underground more enjoyable.

The man raised a small, wooden pipe and blew a low note. All the goldfish leaped up, balancing on their tails and turning in lazy circles. The showman raised the pipe aloft, flourished his arms at the crowd, and the fish dropped gratefully back into their water amid roars and cheers.

"Cute," nodded Emily. "Very cute."

Rob grinned. "Yeah, I've not seen that one before."

I tried to rearrange my facial expression so I didn't look like a gawking country bumpkin. I'd never seen any of it before. I'd never seen a lady levitate, or a huge bouquet of flowers disappear into a matchbox, or fish dance on their tails. When Rob had reminded me that the May Day Fair was rolling into their tiny town and insisted that, this time, I came along, I'd expected a few magic tricks and some rickety rides.

I hadn't expected to be stunned, and bewildered, and dazzled. I hadn't expected to see things that I couldn't believe. And all of it appeared to be for real. If the lady levitated on strings, or wires, she'd certainly fooled me— and trust me, I looked for those wires. After the first few surprises, I tried to relax into it and just enjoy the wonder. Of course horses could be trained to do contortions. Naturally a few quid could buy a fizzing cocktail that changed the colour of my hair.

"Not for ever!" Emily laughed at me. "It'll be back to normal in the morning."

"Just as well." I was certain that the bank would not like cobalt blue on one of their fund managers.

I stared at one impossible thing after another. "I'm trying to play it cool, like I'm not bowled over by everything. But you can see straight through me, right?"

"Literally, there's a stall just over there selling candy floss that makes you transparent."

"There is?"

"No, of course there isn't!" Emily laughed at me again.

"To be fair," added her brother, "there might be. But there never has been before."

I'd been to the town plenty of times before. Rob and I met at university and visited each other's homes in the holidays. His sister was only a year younger, and we'd always got on well. They'd often talked about the May Day Fair, and urged me to join them. Despite their glowing recommendations I'd always declined, imagining a pretty small-scale affair. Happy childhood memories made them return again and again, but for me it was too far to travel for an evening watching a few sideshows. But this year, with the bank holiday falling right afterwards, they'd both insisted I make the journey.

And then they towed me from one stall to another until I felt like my head was about to explode.

"We always told you it was full of marvels!" Emily pointed out.

"Yeah, you did. And I never believed you."

"We could... hey look, it's the Other Life woman! Let's go!"

I had no idea what that meant, but I followed Emily towards a small, square tent with a tall roof. A red-headed teenager on the door queried whether we were all together and asked for five pounds from each of us.

A fiver was pretty steep compared to everything else— I'd only paid two-fifty to see a snake that spat fireworks. But given how excited Emily sounded, I figured it had to be worth it.

"Yes, we'll all come in together," said Rob. "Do you mind?" he checked with me.

"Err... sure." What was there to mind?

"Me first!" Emily ran ahead and sat down on a small wooden chair. An elderly lady, her silver hair twisted into an elaborate knot, ushered Rob and I gently to a sagging floral sofa.

"So," began the lady, her voice dropping almost to a whisper. "Your name is Emily, and you live in Sheffield."

I looked sideways at Rob, waiting to see if he was going to comment. Emily had never, as far as I knew, lived in Sheffield. Rob wasn't looking at me, though, he was staring past his sister at a hillside packed with houses. I stared too, seeing the buildings rush towards me until I was standing inside a large kitchen.

"You are mother to three children," the voice continued, "and wife to Michael Sullivan. You have been married for five years."

Two blonde children tumbled into the kitchen, pursued by someone who was very definitely Emily. She looked a little older, a little heavier, and was smiling as she scooped up the smaller kid for a cuddle.

"You dropped out of university when you discovered you were pregnant. You and Michael had only been dating three months. Later you both decided the baby had probably been conceived the night you got together at Miranda's party."

A thickset man, with a rugby-player's neck, walked into the kitchen carrying another curly blonde tot. He kissed Emily's cheek, before they all faded away.

"You missed this life when you declined a last cocktail and walked home to bed."

The real Emily, our Emily, came back into focus, still sitting on the wooden chair. A smile— a different smile, more wistful— was on her face, but I thought there were tears in her eyes.

She got up and walked slowly over to us but didn't seem to want to say anything. Rob looked at me, eyebrows raised, then headed over to the chair himself.

The lady put her hand on his shoulder and began again. "So, your name is Robert, and you are wondering how you are going to pay your rent."

I almost laughed at that; if there was one thing he absolutely didn't need to worry about, it was where his rent was coming from. But the laugh died as I saw Rob, thin and tired, sitting on a bed in a cramped studio flat.

"People publish your poems, and you command tremendous respect in literary circles. You speak at exclusive events, where hushed audiences hang on your every word. But the money is terrible."

Rob picked up a small book, in a beautiful grey binding, and turned it over. *A Summer's Life*, by Robert Collier.

"Your first collection has just been published. Perhaps it will make your fortune. You have been working towards that book for two and half years.

"You missed this life the day you took the job at the ad agency."

The bedsit melted away, leaving Rob on the wooden chair, looking a little shell-shocked. He stayed there, his eyes lost in a distance I couldn't see.

I looked at Emily. "What is this, exactly? A kind of fortune telling? For might-have-been fortunes?" I whispered, trying not to break the silence.

Emily shrugged. "It's the story of another life. One you didn't live. One you could have lived, if you'd made a different choice somewhere. A big choice, like turning down a job, or a tiny one like deciding you'd already had one drink too many."

"And you want to know about these other lives?"

"Of course! Aren't you curious? About the other versions of you out there? Don't you want to know if they're happy? Sad? Regretting their choice?"

I hadn't ever thought about it. "I guess so."

Rob moved quietly over to the side of the tent, and I sat down.

"So..."

As the lady began to speak, I felt a blind, irrational panic well up inside me. What if every other version of me was doing better? What if every choice I'd ever regretted would have made me happier, richer?

Rob and Emily had both seen other selves who were living

different, but fulfilling, lives. I feared seeing another, more successful me— but what if I saw myself hopeless, or starving, or in prison?

"Your name..."

I wasn't actually sure I wanted to go through with this.

"Your name..."

The scene around me did not shift. The sagging, white wall of the tent remained in place, and I could hear an uncomfortable wheezing as the elderly lady tried to keep her breathing under control. She sounded like she'd been running: gasping, unable to get out the words.

I didn't want to hear what she had to say.

"Your name is..."

I looked directly towards her, and saw her eyes round with terror, her pupils tiny dots of ink. She staggered away, blurting "I'm sorry."

"Huh?"

"I have no other life for you."

"What? What do you mean?"

"Ask Raf for your money back. He'll give you double. I am sorry." Her hands were gesturing, flapping, almost shoving me towards the door. Confused, I hurried out, not even remembering to ask the teenager for my refund.

Outside, the three of us stared at each other.

Eventually I broke the silence. "Is this some kind of joke?"

"No!"

"Of course not!"

They both started talking at once, then both stopped.

"I'm sorry," said Rob. "I don't know what happened there."

None of us said anything, but we all started walking away from the May Day Fair, back to Rob's family home.

Although I'd been on the point of pushing the old woman aside, leaving, telling her that I didn't want to hear about another me, I now couldn't stop wondering. What might I have seen? Perhaps a self where I went to a different university and didn't meet Rob, or the self who asked Emily out that summer I was twenty. Or the self that decided it was too far to travel up to the Fair.

Would any of those decisions have made a difference? How many other lives did a person have?

We sat round the table in Rob's mum's kitchen, drinking tea and whisky. But the conversation was awkward, and no one mentioned what had happened. Pretty soon we all headed off to bed.

I lay awake for a long time, wondering if the other selves that Rob and Emily had seen were pretty fantasies, or real people living their own lives. Perhaps mother-of-three Emily went home to the May Day Fair and saw instead a ferociously-driven, eager veterinary science student living in a tiny flat with nothing but textbooks to keep her company in the evenings. Perhaps mother-of-three Emily never existed.

I slept badly. I woke often, and eventually in the early hours I got up, got dressed, and let myself out of the house.

I walked back towards the common and found people already

stirring. Tents were being struck, wagons packed, and horses harnessed. There were motor vehicles too, of course, but many of these people still travelled with horse-drawn caravans.

I headed straight towards the spot I thought the Other Life tent had been, although it was gone. I looked around, trying to get my bearings among the half-dismantled sideshows.

Someone walked past me, furled in an ancient brown dressing gown and hurrying along head-down. A long, silver plait hung over one shoulder, and I realised that yes, surely, this was the woman.

"Hey!"

She didn't turn around.

I ran after her, tapping her on the shoulder. "Excuse me!"

She stopped, but still didn't look at me. "You."

"Yes, me. Why wouldn't you show me another life?"

Her shoulders sagged. "I'm sorry, I couldn't."

"Why not?"

"I try to show people a positive life, something they will enjoy. I don't show your friend Rob the life where he dies of hepatitis, I don't show his sister the life where the man walks out on her and the baby. I couldn't see something I thought you would enjoy."

"My other lives were all unhappy?"

She looked at me, staring directly into my eyes in a way that scared me. "In every other life I could see you were already dead."

She turned away and was already a few paces back towards her caravan before I found a response.

"Dead? All of them? Why? How often does this happen? What does it mean?"

"I don't know. I don't know." She was still walking, hurrying, trying to leave me behind.

"Does it mean I will die soon? Will I...?"

"I don't know! Perhaps you are strong and bold and determined. Perhaps you are doomed. I don't know!" Her voice shook, and her already-pale face looked waxy in the morning sunlight. She stormed away and I let her go, watching her silver hair swing down her back.

What Has Waited Between the Stars

Daphne Fama

Daphne Fama has split her life between the Philippines, Korea, and the USA. In that time she's been transfixed by the unmoving stars and the rapid change of the Earth. To deal with the existential dread both give her she's become a nonprofit attorney. You can find her short stories in a smattering of places online.

My mouth is full of blood and dirt and rock. I move my jaw, and it pops. Jagged shards of pain lance up my neck and burrow into my skull, into the shaken grey matter that throbs beneath that bone plating. The pain stays in the space between my ears, a bolt of lightning that grows roots, digging deep, until I have to question who I am. Where I am. What I've become. There is no part of my head that doesn't feel like it isn't on fire.

I am not dead. I wish I was.

The pain overwhelms and forces me back to blackness, and I go without a fight. When I feel again, the pain is duller. The blood is no longer fresh. The dirt is a thick paste on the roof of my mouth.

Pus tries to keep my eyelashes glued together. But I force them apart, and a pale lilac sky peers back between the broken shards of my visor. My suit has been shorn apart. I gasp for breath, inhale dirt and bits of teeth, cough. Exhale, expel, inhale, repeat.

The atmosphere is breathable. It shouldn't be, and every breath comes with effort. There should be nothing here at all. And yet it's a planet beneath my feet, an alien sky above my head, strange dirt between my teeth. It exists where radars read empty space, interrupted only by meteors, dust, and radiation.

I hadn't even been at the controls. The ship flew on autopilot while I pored over the letters of the woman I loved. Missives that told me she loved me but hated what I'd done. That by the time

I came back she'd be old, and I'd still be the woman she met by chance in a bar only to sweep her off her feet.

But I'd left, anyway. Not to be cruel. But because the pull of the stars had always been stronger than any Earth's delight, than even the promise of soulmates. And now here I was, stranded. My ship nowhere to be seen, the surrounding land unmarred by the destruction of a crash landing. But it must have crashed, because my visor is broken, and my teeth are shattered, and my head aches. I can't even recall why I am wearing a spacesuit. It doesn't fit; it isn't mine.

It takes me an hour to pull myself into a sitting position. Another twenty to peel off the layers of protective gear until only the thin, synthetic skinsuit clings to me.

With trembling fingers and split nails, I pluck bits of metal from my skin. It pockmarks my shins, my thighs, my stomach. There is more in my shoulder and face, I am certain of it. I can feel it every time I breathe, every time I instinctively work my jaw back and forth, just to hear it click.

Finally, I gather my courage. I take stake of my surroundings.

There is something akin to trees that stab into the lavender skies, dotting the landscape by the dozens. Their trunks are pale white obelisks. Segmented and geometric, tapering into a soft, pliant webbing that pushes into the earth like roots. The higher the obelisks go, the more they thin and then branch off, creating bismuth-like growths that spread out like plantain leaves.

There is smaller, not precisely organic, life scattered here and there at the base of these pillars. They are bulbous and bowl-like, the inside of them full of thin razor-sharp gills, like the belly beneath a mushroom cap. The gills move in a wavelike formation, elegant and in synch.

I touch nothing. My mouth is still coated in dirt. It is a well of sand, my tongue a dried slab of meat. Hunger grows in the bottom of my stomach, but worst is the dehydration. I can almost feel my skin thinning, tightening, becoming a husk in the dry air. In this place without vegetation or water, where everything springs from hard-packed rock.

I wander. The sky stretches above me, lavender, touched with pale blue mists. The mist coils and unfurls, dissipates and gathers, until it's almost opaque as clouds. It does so in random intervals, so that it's impossible to determine a pattern or motive.

I trained for this my entire life. Since they told us Earth's extinction was years, not decades away. When the water supply ran out, and the fish died in their beds, and the people turned on their own, and the last best hope was amongst the stars.

We had discovered countless planets before, landed and gotten our feet dirty. But the life there was minimal. Great expanses of dust, or gas, or liquid so hot or cold as to be inhospitable. But this is something else entirely. There is no field guide for this, beyond touch nothing. Breathe nothing.

My lungs filled with its air. My stomach, its dirt. I wasn't certain that it was even my ship that had embedded its metal into me.

I wander. The great star above does not move. The day does not set. There is no night, no passage of time. But the hunger grows. I stumble amongst the obelisks, searching for the remnants of my ship. For some semblance of the familiar, of something that might pass for home.

Countless times I stumble, my knees hitting the ground until the

173

skinsuit breaches. Until the skin beneath wears away. Until I am dripping blood. In desperation I cut at the gills of the strange growths beneath the obelisks, only for them to crumble away into a dust. Delirious, half-mad, I stagger and crawl. Perhaps I have walked the entire length of this planet. Perhaps the planet rolls backward, so I have not moved at all.

On the horizon, something glimmers. The soft mists settle onto the hills. In it, a glow undulates, flickering and beckoning. Beckoning, I know, for me.

There is no other sound than my own exhausted, rasping breath and my dragging feet as I force my body forward. As if the glow is a lodestar. My last chance of survival or purpose.

The soft blue leans towards me, its glow dancing between the gray. Each step takes me closer, and the air grows denser, until the mist wraps itself around me. It's like walking into the fogs that filled the valleys outside of my hometown. The air is thick and sticky. It fills my nose, my mouth, and the taste is morning dew. Nothing like the acrid taste of burning plastic I'd grown up with.

No, this is clean and pure.

My tongue extends, and I breathe deep, desperate to drown in it. It fills me, slipping deeper into the cavern of my throat, until all I can think of is its taste. But it withdraws from me. The mist sweeps back. My eyes flutter open, my lips already forming a protest.

But words die because she is here.

She looks like Cassandra if she'd been carved from galaxies. Her skin is incandescent, almost the same lavender as the sky. The mist pools into her, then out, as if it is her breath. I take a hesitant step towards her, the way you might approach a deer dappled in moonlight, in awe of its natural beauty, in fear that you might ruin the moment. But drawn forward, nonetheless.

"Cassandra?"

I say her name, though of course it's not her. The closer I come, the more apparent it is. She does not have Cassandra's lilting smile, the cocky lift of a brow, as if she knows something you don't. The face of the creature or thing before me is a series of flickering projections over what I now see is a smooth caprice, something that approximates a woman's body. But what pretty lights they are. How close to her image they are.

Cassandra beckons, and her hands are human enough. They are missing fingers, there are no fingers at all. Just a sort of rectangular webbing, stretched across two prongs. I reach back, and faster than I know it, I am in her embrace again. Her blue mists expel outwards from the vents in her caprice, probing at my lips. And again I let her in, this time leaning towards her, towards the smooth neck that could have been Cassandra's.

The earth slopes away beneath our feet. I see now that her own legs extend deep into the crust. She is like an obelisk, a pillar of stone, whose roots might reach the center of the planet. But as the ground gives way, she holds onto me. Her arms are strong and unrelenting, and I know we are safe as we descend, intertwined, into the earth. Into a network of roots that extends just below the surface, sticky and thick, vibrating with a life-force that I know will be mine.

The earth buries me, inch by inch, and the roots crawl upward, engulfing us.

Those closest to me begin to peel until they are covered with something like trichobothria: the fine hairs on a spider's arm.

And then those razor-sharp hairs are in me. Pricking me at every surface. My throat tries a scream, but the mouth has piled too high onto my tongue, between my teeth. Even a muffled groan is beyond me.

The hairs of the root drill fine holes and work their way into my skin, into my bloodstream and bone.

Cassandra hums inside my veins.

Her song has no words.

We've gone so far beyond that.

There is no separation between what she thinks and what I think. We are two shades of gray, two breaths of strange, foreign air, intermingling together in the mists that were built in this soil, in the atmosphere that had been tailor made for the body I had once been.

My hunger becomes her hunger, and we are insatiable. Delicate synapses, marrow, a menagerie of hormones and liquids and flesh. We devour ourselves, morsel by morsel. Milligram by milligram because there is no sating this emptiness and there is no telling when the next meal will come. So, we may as well take our time.

Thin filaments run the length of our body. We become the exo-skeleton, the brain, the neurons from which its malignant intelligence alight. It stretches arms thin; it pulls skintight. In the eons to come, this body will become an obelisk, like those who came before it. An unmarked tombstone for the unremembered and unmourned.

We—It—will forget that there was ever a life before this everlasting pain of slow devouring. But until then, we dig into this new brain, pulling forth memories of places it wished it had known, before the great cataclysm reduced what had been a beautiful country to dust. The dense jungles of the Philippines, its rolling hills, its vast oceans.

Then, next, even more succulent than dreams come the memories. The sweet and the bitter and the mundane. Each more tender than the last.

Cassandra in a dive bar. Cassandra in a bed. Cassandra on a doorstep of a house that We—She—It refused to call home. A compendium of other faces. Coworkers and family and friends.

For the next human, we will be able to replicate a perfect copy. A lure to mingle with our cerulean breath, until they are pliant in our mouth. But for now, our crust contracts. Our purple skies give way to an airless vacuum of space. We pull ourselves tight and small, until we are an asteroid, hurtling through space amongst one hundred thousand others.

We cast wide a net that can't be perceived with light. Strange, vibrating threads of a web that anchor to the nearby stars, which are younger still than We.

Another ship will come. Maybe not for another millennium. But we will exist long after the sun bursts and a new one is born in its place. Until new life comes to seek something in the void.

State Vs. Hades

Altaire Gural

A member of the Playwrights Guild of Canada, Altaire's original play Forgotten has been performed all over the world. Her speculative short stories have appeared in the anthologies Matters of Time, and Kawartha Writers, and also she coaches professional actors for film and television.

CRIMINAL DISTRICT COURT
ELEUSIS

STATE
Versus
HADES

Probable Cause Hearing

Testimony and Notes of Evidence, taken in the above-entitled and -numbered cause, before the **HON. THEMIS, Judge**, presiding.

APPEARANCES:

REPRESENTING THE STATE:

DEMOSTHENES,
ORATOR FOR THE PROSECUTION

AESCHINES
ORATOR FOR THE DEFENSE

Witness Index

Demeter
Sea Nymph
Therapist
Charon
Zeus

DEMOSTHENES: Your Honor, the State is ready to proceed with motions in the case against Hades.

AESCHINES: Your Honor, Aeschines on behalf of Hades.

THEMIS: This is the matter of the State versus Hades.

AESCHINES: Yes. Hades is present in the court and we're ready for motions.

THEMIS: Very well. Call your first witness.

I would that the earth swallowed me all over again, Mother. You say this is not my fault, but I feel so completely responsible. The looks others give me; I might die of the shame.

DEMOSTHENES: For the record, you are Kore?

PERSEPHONE: Yes.

DEMOSTHENES: The maiden?

PERSEPHONE: Not anymore.

DEMOSTHENES: On the day in question, you were playing in a field?

PERSEPHONE: I was gathering flowers.

DEMOSTHENES: And you'd wandered away from the sea nymphs who were looking after you?

PERSEPHONE: I'm a big girl.

DEMOSTHENES: Can you explain what happened next? While you were gathering flowers?

I didn't want to play by the edge of the ocean. I didn't want to hear the lovely chatter of the nymphs any longer; they talk lightly because, for the most part, they live in the deep. They save their words for idleness, which I suppose is like holding your breath for so long that eventually it bursts from your lungs, and you can't help but laugh. I didn't want to laugh.

I didn't want to talk. I wanted a moment to myself, to think, or not remotely to have a thought in my head at all. I was searching for me while I searched for the flowers. I stayed in this attitude for the entirety of the morning, breathing in the fragrance of the meadow, sharing the environment with the butterflies that danced around me.

And then an intolerable sound, as if the earth were keening, and I lost my footing, while startled birds took flight.

It wasn't just that the ground shook. The very air was shaking, blurring out the clouds as if the shadows that sprung from the chasm in front of me had risen up to blot out the sun. And before me stood a great cart, very different from the one belonging to Phoebus, blocking my view of the dunes, and driven by horses that could only be born of night.

AESCHINES: What were you doing by yourself, alone in an empty field? You were told to stay with your friends.

PERSEPHONE: Within the confines of four walls, what hope do we have? Even in a field of nothing but sun and flowers, their gaze finds us.

AESCHINES: Was it all exciting? This attention, the spectacle of that first moment?

PERSEPHONE: ...It was...

AESCHINES: I suppose you could say you felt the earth move?

...I'll have that smirk wiped from your face...

DEMOSTHENES: The Defense is leading my witness, your Honor!

I often wonder: did I say anything, do anything to incite attention? I wrack my mind, and go over every tiny detail till I've unraveled those memories beyond recognition. I can think of nothing. And yet...I must have?

The nymphs talk of love and its fragile nature, how it recedes before it's begun in proper. I did not know love. I knew agape, Mother, like you taught me. For all. All of them.

I never mentioned how he'd look at me, or sit me on his knee, or the way he'd place his hand at my hip. Reunions would never be right if I did, ever again. You and I both know that. You knew that before, I think.

And yet you brought me anyway. And you did not see. And yOu DiD nOt SeE.

AESCHINES: And on the day in question, did you see anything at all?

NYMPH: No, Sir.

AESCHINES: Nothing?

NYMPH: We was at the sea, Sir. It's hard to see beyond the beach, considering.

AESCHINES: Considering you have tails...

NYMPH: Yes, Sir.

AESCHINES: But you heard screaming.

NYMPH: I don't know what I heard, Sir. I wasn't sure.

I didn't scream. I didn't. I'm certain there was a good reason at the time, but I just can't seem to remember why. I do recall thinking he did not choose the other girls, he chose me.

They press their fingers into our flesh, their breath into our mouths, their ideas into our minds so there is little room again for our own thoughts.

And I'm not sure why.

AESCHINES: I'm given to understand that there is no one that comes to Tartarus that does not meet you first, is this true?

THEMIS: The witness will answer, not just nod his head...

CHARON: Yes, that's right. That's correct.

AESCHINES: You saw the young lady there, Kore?

CHARON: Not at first.

AESCHINES: But you did meet her.

CHARON: A lovely young lady, without question.

AESCHINES: Has she ever...has she ever seemed, I don't know...unhappy to you?

CHARON: Far from it! Miss Kore always seemed *most* happy. Why, any young woman should be so lucky to live in a place like our underworld. The palace is beautiful, all covered in shining gems

like rubies and diamonds, shaped into poppies
and narcissi. It's a right dream.

*Do you remember, Mother, sharing all the names of the flowers
with me? And showing me how to plant the seeds so that eventually they'd become bulbs, and then burst into stalks, then blos-
soms? Do you remember telling me to close my eyes, and name
the smell of each flower you waved in front of me? I remember.
You would take me by the hand, and show me all the places where
life would grow, and you'd tell me it's all creation, and beauty,
and that one day I would know creation too. I was simply happy
to follow you around, hearing the people call to you in joy as we
passed by. But then I was so little.*

DEMOSTHENES: Was she a good child? Well behaved?

DEMETER: Oh, yes! She was the loveliest, kindest...

DEMOSTHENES: Never talked back?

DEMETER: No, not at all.

*You train us to do as we're told, and that somehow this is the mark
of a woman of decorum and honor. You teach us to say yes, and
then spend the rest of our lives telling us we should learn to say no.
No is a word of power, Mother. You did not protect me. You left
me vulnerable. You made me prey.*

DEMOSTHENES: How does Persephone's behavior seem
    now that she's returned to you?

DEMETER: ...she's not herself.

DEMOSTHENES: I'll need you to give me more details
    about that

DEMETER: She's short tempered. That's not like her at all. That's never been her.

DEMOSTHENES: Go on…

DEMETER: She stays in her room now, and keeps the curtains closed at her window. I came in once to open them, to let fresh air in, and she screamed at me. She hadn't even gotten out of bed yet.

DEMOSTHENES: Well, to be honest, this seems like normal youth behavior "of an age."

DEMETER: …she called me a "bitch."

DEMOSTHENES: Forgive me, but that seems like normal teenage fare as well?

DEMETER: She then screamed something about "the Lie of the promise of regeneration…"

I'm sorry I said all that. I regretted it the second it was out of my mouth.

Do you remember when you cut an apple in half on its side, and you showed me that the core and the seeds are in the shape of a star? The first time you showed me that, I knew there was magic in the world that was both simple, and greater than the overwhelm of us.

I've spent long hours sitting hidden in the tall grasses, thinking about the seeds in the stars, staring at the sky as if it's all apples cut sideways.

I could eat the whole universe.

Truth be told, I always shock myself with these thoughts. I've no

idea where this comes from, this wanting to expand beyond my
smallness. I want to be bigger than the moon, greater than the sun,
swallowing all the stars, and thinking of none of the things that
bog the rest of you down.

I want to fly apart. I've tried, mother. Did you know?

DEMOSTHENES: Were you scared?

DEMETER: Terrified. I had no idea where she was, or what
        she was going through.

I wandered for days, beneath the weight of the high vaulted ceil-
ings, down long corridors made of amethyst, shining as though
they were mirrors, my hands running along the smooth surfaces.
Sometimes I saw faces buried within those walls, but they fol-
lowed me, like a ghostly retinue, and I was never alone. Again.
Above and below, I had no peace. I found bracelets by my bed-
side table each morning, cut geodes resembling the rinds of
watermelon, the gems ragged. I'd press the sharpness of them to
my skin to watch blood well up. I'd sit there, in a daze, and then
I'd smash the bracelets. But always the next morning, there were
more bracelets on the table.

Do you know what I did, Mother? I went to seek playmates. But
here they all slithered, or cried, or...fell apart, their limbs falling in
pieces to the floor. These are not the normal playmates of youth,
the serpents, and the dead. They think differently, they speak dif-
ferently. They told me of "before," and it seems the ones that had
truly and desperately lived before they died...did things, sought
out those paths that led to adventure! I understood them. And I
now knew why gathering flowers would not suffice. Some people
love the view of smooth stones, some ragged. I suppose you can
tell which one I am. Eventually, I came to understand that world
too. The Underworld is a haunted place, and the haunted are not

frightened; they're lost, wandering, unsure, with no clear pur-
pose. Purpose is mankind's driving force, and to have none is an
unimaginable suffering.

Many are lost, like I am, and I see that these are my people.

The lost never have tomorrow. It's all a vast sea of now, and it's
endless. They rail against the knowledge of this neverending, and
this is where the mind cracks, like the fissures in the heated rock
beneath the earth. I've touched my hand to those fissures, feeling
the split as it widens and then narrows. I cannot touch my mind,
though. I don't know if anyone can.

I think my mind is broken, Mother.

AESCHINES: You work long hours?

DEMETER: Yes.

AESCHINES: Seasonal work, am I right? It requires you to
    be away from your home for long stretches.

DEMETER: I *am* the goddess of the harvest, so yes.

AESCHINES: You're also a mother.

DEMOSTHENES: Is that a question?

AESCHINES: So who stays home with the children when
    you're away?

DEMETER: I'm home for dinner each night.

AESCHINES: And the rest of the 23 hours. Who is
    with them?

DEMETER: I have people I trust.

AESCHINES: Sea nymphs.

DEMETER: …yes.

AESCHINES: Reliable, are they?

DEMETER: They're wonderful girls.

AESCHINES: Who was looking after your daughter the day she "went missing?"

(You thought you'd watch over the entire world, and you forgot to watch over me. And I did hate you for that. I did. Can we forgive each other now)?

AESCHINES: You could not make your marriage work?

DEMETER: We were never married.

AESCHINES: And why is that?

DEMOSTHENES: How is this relevant?

THEMIS: The witness will answer the question.

DEMETER: …He was married already.

AESCHINES: Ah. I see. You were sleeping with a married man.

DEMETER: It's not like that. I had no interest in a relationship.

AESCHINES: Just a quick fling, amiright? I get it.

DEMOSTHENES: Your Honor…

THEMIS: That last comment from the Defense will be stricken from the record.

You're angry, Mother. I see it. It's everywhere, the ground rough and unyielding beneath my feet, the land cold and brittle so that little birds fall, lifeless, from their perches. The wildness in the world has become formal, inflexible. Hard. Please don't become hard, Mother. Or was it that I was your softness all along?

I heard the children crying from hunger, clutching their bellies to ease the pain. And their mothers and fathers, those same people who waved to us in the fields as we passed, blowing kisses and showering us with rose petals -those same fathers and mothers holding their children to them as they suffer, knowing that their prayers were unheard, and their children lost.

You starved the children, mother!

I do not know this side of you. Perhaps this is what it is to be a god? To feel so little for those we reign over, to be a creature devoid of reason. This gnashing of teeth is far too late, but does it make it well, Mother? Do you feel justified? Vindicated? Does this alleviate your guilt?

I see your guilt, too. In part, I am glad of it. Until I recognize your guilt serves you, and no one else. I waited, and I wAiTeD, and you never came. And I was starving too.

You could have warned me, you know. Prepared me for every monster around every turn and every corner. And the world is all corners. You might at least have told me about one or two of those monsters, and what the face of this story truly looks like.

You chose instead to let me walk the world unfettered by fear.

I cannot tell which is the better way. I cannot tell which I would do for my own children. I suppose when my mistakes come, I'll know I should have done differently then.

DEMOSTHENES: Tell me about the family dynamic.

THERAPIST L.C.P.C: These circumstances were not completely unexpected.

DEMOSTHENES: Care to explain?

THERAPIST L.C.P.C: An absentee father. A father in name only. Present when it suits his purpose. The Weekend Fun Dad, if you will.

DEMETER: Not even that!

THEMIS: Order!

DEMOSTHENES: A mother, overworked, rarely home.

THERAPIST L.C.P.C: The burden often falls to the mother.

DEMOSTHENES: Haven't we all moved away from that thinking?...Could you please clarify, for the Court, because we can't hear the look you're giving me.

THERAPIST L.C.P.C.: This situation is also...unique...in that the family dynamic is entangled.

DEMOSTHENES: Entangled. Please explain what you mean.

THERAPIST L.C.P.C.: Well...they're all related. It's a whole other level of complicated...

DEMOSTHENES: Isn't the Egyptian pantheon also -

THERAPIST L.C.P.C: Don't even get me started...

DEMOSTHENES: Alright. This family's entanglement...

THERAPIST L.C.P.C.: There's co-dependence, and a clear form of the Drama Triangle happening here.

DEMOSTHENES: Yes, the Drama Triangle. Please explain that here for us as well. I've heard a bit about it…

You were all so busy, running around, being very official and important. What have you all been trying to prove all this time? You've left no room for healing, no room for family. And when you don't get your own way?…there is zero room for trust.

DEMOSTHENES: Are you close with your daughter?

ZEUS: I am a proud papa.

What's my favourite flower, Father?

AESCHINES: Are you supportive of this alliance? Between Hades and Kore?

ZEUS: She would be well taken care of. He is profoundly well off. He's probably wealthier than I am!

AESCHINES: So you're saying she was after the money.

ZEUS: Well. You know how they are. Shower of gold, and all that…

AESCHINES: I take your meaning.

I've never understood your role as my father. Isn't that strange? I did not understand how she could touch you. Oh, I understood the physical of it…I'd seen the act between field beasts. Mother explained to me one day the necessity in order for continuation. She explained lineages, bloodlines, what decent sires and mares were, how they produced, and then what young beasts needed to eat in order to thrive.

I looked at all the young in the wild. They needed their sires as little as I needed you. You rarely spoke to me, or acknowledged me. And when you did see me...it was clear I was measured.

I always hoped she wouldn't fall for your act -you know the act I mean. The one you're doing right now, winking at the stenographer -she always fell for it, though. I'd run to the meadows so that I didn't have to hear you both, because the walls are thinner than you can imagine.

It's all just spreading seeds, it seems. Life casting seeds of every kind

Also, presence over presents, you Fuck.

DEMOSTHENES: Did you ever encounter Kore outside of family functions?

HADES: Not often.

DEMOSTHENES: So you have?

HADES: I would see her as I took my dog for a walk. I'd bump into her, gathering flowers.

DEMOSTHENES: "Bumped into her." Completely by chance, I assume?

HADES: I was not stalking her.

DEMOSTHENES: You did not choose her because she was affable? Compliant?

HADES: ...She seemed...

DEMOSTHENES: Yes?

HADES: Lonely.

DEMOSTHENES: You did not speak to her mother of your concerns? You took it upon yourself to make judgements?

HADES: I saw that she was-

DEMOSTHENES: ...a child?

HADES: An ally. I saw an ally. I could tell that she viewed things the way I did, before she'd even set foot in my realm. She understood concepts that people do not normally grasp.

DEMOSTHENES: Indeed? That hardly seems likely.

HADES: She understood the nature of the Curtain. She understood the nature of death.

DEMOSTHENES: Doesn't everyone? It's the "end."

HADES: No. It takes a unique mind to comprehend the alien quality of the metaphysics of death.

DEMOSTHENES: The metaphysics of death? My, that sounds..."deep."

HADES: You cannot know. Your mind would break. To you, it would be terrifying.

DEMOSTHENES: How convenient. Tell me...was she mature for her age? Wise beyond her years? Not like "other girls?"

HADES: Go fuck yourself.

DEMOSTHENES: ...Sounds like that's what you should have done.

THEMIS: Order!

I was lonely. I didn't think I was, but it's true. I was lonely for my own identity, and my own thoughts. I'm not always an extension of you.

Oh, Mother. You think that I am returned to you. That I am present.

He did make me feel unique, at first. I felt in control. It's quite something to have power over the powerful. I came to align with his Destruction, because you are Creation. How else does a girl rebel? But...

His mind is broken into a million little pieces, and he thought I could help him put it back together again. I cannot do that. In my heart I know, in my mind I'll always be looking at the sky, larger than the moon, greater than the sun. Eating all the stars so that I'm the shining one. Other. Cosmically whole.

In this world that values spring, where I resemble spring on the outside, on the inside I am winter.

You both tear at me between your realms. I cannot stand in your world, Mother, and I cannot stand in his. I didn't want to eat the seeds, but they looked like rubies, and I was starving, and there were no stars...

But it's not six months of the year. It's the entire year. It occupies my mind the entire year. And so it will forever.

Earth Report

Hannah Whiteoak

Hannah Whiteoak is a writer of speculative short fiction and flash. Her work has appeared in Flash Fiction Online, Escape Pod, On The Premises, and various anthologies. Find her online at www.hannahwhiteoak.me or @hannahwhiteoak

This story first appeared in Asymmetry Fiction, December 2018.

Nothing exemplifies human pettiness more than a Sunday morning trip to the supermarket. People waddle through the aisles, bickering with their families. They cluster around the shelf of reduced items, shoving strangers out of the way, fingers reaching greedily for cut-price cream cakes and punnets of half-rotten strawberries. When I prepare my report for the committee, these Sunday morning shopping trips will supply a large part of the evidence I need to justify my conclusion that humans do not qualify for protection under the Mature Species Preservation Act.

In my disguise as an unhappily married, middle-aged man who is running to fat around the middle, I tell my daughter to put the ice cream back in the freezer. I say "my daughter," but of course she is not. Her father's consciousness has been suppressed, leaving his body free for me to use while I conduct my investigations into Earth life.

Dr. Bennington taught science to human children aged between eleven and sixteen Earth years, an occupation I have continued since taking over his body. By "science," I of course mean falsehoods derived by human scientists, erroneous concepts such as quantum physics and the orbital model of the atom. My investigations suggest he didn't much like the job, although I assume he, like the rest of the human species, was ignorant of the scientific errors in the material he taught. As he also seems not to be too fond of his wife, Catherine, or his daughter, Ginny, it appears the committee did him a favour by freeing up his body for a higher purpose.

Dr. Bennington's daughter is thirteen, in that awkward phase between juvenile and adult. In denim short-shorts, she is all legs. When I tell her she can't have ice cream, she rolls her eyes and dumps the carton on a shelf, where it will spoil. In the same gap on the shelf (the store has somehow sold its entire stock of tinned mackerel) is a frozen pork shoulder. I have yet to work out whether humans dump food like this out of spite—yet another example of their "if I can't have it no one can" mentality—or simple laziness. In Ginny's case, I suspect both motives apply.

"Put it back," I tell her.

Ginny pretends not to hear me, feigning interest in the many rows of tinned tuna. I take the ice cream back to the freezer myself, manoeuvring the trolley with difficulty. Despite having discovered electromagnetism hundreds of years ago, humans still haven't implemented levitation technology and instead rely on wheels. Yes, wheels! A Slime Age technology.

One of the things that makes supermarkets so awful on Sundays is that they aren't allowed to open until 11am, and they close at 5pm. This is something to do with religion, which is a uniquely human obsession. Whereas other intelligent species have applied themselves to finding technological solutions for mortality, often with very good results, humans have instead constructed a make-believe place called heaven to make themselves feel better about dying. There are no fewer than 4,200 human religions devoted to fleshing out this belief, and all of them have their own set of bizarre rules. The particular religion that once dominated the damp little island to which I have been assigned insists that humans do nothing useful on Sundays. Even though very few of the inhabitants still cling to this belief system, no one has bothered to repeal the law that restricts shops to opening only certain hours on a Sunday. By the time 11am rolls around, human greed and impatience have built up, creating a mass of hungry people ready to elbow each other out of the way to get the last fresh loaf.

None of the other members of my "family" seem to mind the delay. On Sundays, they indulge in a "lie in," which involves sleeping for an obscenely long time. I do not sleep. I stare at the ceiling, feeling exhausted, wishing I could be among my own kind. I am so lonely.

My wife returns from the produce section clutching two bags of kale. Humans have an enviable ability to thrive on an extremely wide variety of diets, and yet an astonishing number of them are convinced they must eat "superfoods" or suffer some ill-defined malaise. Catherine is one of these people. Every evening she inputs her day's intake into a piece of computer software that tells her she's consumed 10mg too little calcium and five percent too much saturated fat. I point out that the daily amounts the human scientists recommend are based on guesswork, but it does no good. She can spend hours looking for the perfect combination of foods to address the imbalance.

It is sad to see a human waste her short life this way. If Catherine would only apply her industriousness to something useful, she could be a decent observer for the Species Preservation Service. She'll never get the chance, of course. Over the last three months, I've gathered all the evidence I need to say that humans' redeeming qualities do not outweigh their many flaws. When the planet they call Earth is vaporised during the construction of the new wormhole transportation service, no humans will be taken to a reserve for preservation. Instead, resources will be diverted to saving more worthy species. Personally, I have high hopes for the

X'Chulthula, a slime-based species of cannibal worms with a surprisingly rich and complex culture.

"I had to fight for these," says Catherine. "Some woman tried to tell me I didn't need two bags, and tried to take one from my basket. Can you imagine?"

I can imagine. Theft is an integral part of human culture.

Ginny is now trying to convince her mother to buy her a magazine. This is a variation on the ancient human technology of books, but instead of useful or even entertaining content, the pages are filled with articles telling human women they are not pretty enough (amazing as it may seem, humans do sometimes consider each other attractive) and advertisements for mostly ineffective products that are supposed to fix the flaws.

"Tell her, Harry," Catherine says. "I can't argue with her anymore."

"No magazines," I say. "And that's final."

It's surprisingly easy, pretending to be Dr. Bennington. I smile when people expect me to smile, say "Oh, fine," when anyone asks me how I am, and pretend to care about those close to me. Sometimes I wonder whether humans are actually like this, cold inside, and their displays of emotion—the songs, poems, paintings—are fake.

The next part of the shopping trip is the only bright spot. We head to the biscuit aisle, where Catherine allows Ginny and I to each pick out a single packet. For those unfamiliar with human culture, a biscuit is a small, hard-baked wheat product. They are divine. My favourite consists of a sweet layer of chocolate cream sandwiched between two chocolate wafers. When I bite into one, I forget for a moment that I don't belong on this planet. I forget that I am alone. I even forget my plan to dispose of the useless body in which I am trapped. It's a mystery to me why any human ever does anything other than eat biscuits. I've yet to meet a person who doesn't cheer up at least a little while crunching one.

Next, the most arduous part: the checkout. As we join the queue, which tails back into the aisle so shoppers who are still collecting their goods have to push their way between us, another family's small boy is screaming. I wish humans could close their ears. At least I'll be getting out of here tomorrow. I have it all planned out. Instead of going to work, I'll drive to the pass that winds along the side of a hill and, instead of slowing down as the signs suggest, speed up until I smash through the barriers, hurling the car into open air. My consciousness will be beamed back home, while Dr. Bennington's body will be crushed between seat and steering wheel as the car nose-dives onto the rocks.

I won't be sorry to be rid of this body. It always seems to be hungry or hot, cold or tired. The knees are creaky, in dire need of regenerative therapy. Prickly hair grows from the nostrils and ears; trimming it back is a constant battle.

The queue inches forward. The small boy, who stopped crying when his father threatened to "give him something to cry about," is now squirming and whining that he needs to go to the toilet. Every time he tries to squat down, his mother yanks him up by the arm.

Finally, the family pays for their shopping and leaves. We step forward. I am ready. When the cashier passes the items through, I pile them into the trolley, keeping pace with her breakneck scanning. This isn't even my planet, and I still manage this process better than the idiots who try to pack their items into bags at the checkout. Ginny and Catherine are still arguing about the magazine.

I tell the cashier I'll pay by card before she even asks. I reach into my back pocket for my wallet. My pocket is empty. I remember seeing my wallet sitting on my bedside table. Did I really forget to pick it up this morning?

"Where's my wallet?" I ask Catherine.

"I don't know. Have you checked your pockets?"

"Yes." I pat them down again to confirm. "It's not here. You'll have to pay."

"I can't. I didn't bring my purse. You always pay."

We both look at Ginny. "Don't look at me!" she says indignantly. "Why would I carry a wallet? It's not like you give me any pocket money to put in it."

"Honestly, Harry," Catherine says. "How could you forget? We're going to have to go all the way home, and by the time we get there and back again, the salmon will have defrosted. And someone will steal the kale. I got the last two bags in the store!"

She looks like she's about to cry. I feel her pain in my chest: dull and nauseating, as though someone has kicked me in the breastbone. Although I'm sure I have never before felt what humans call empathy, the sensation is strangely familiar. And there is absolutely nothing I can do about it. How could I know how to comfort a human?

"Excuse me," says a voice behind me. Do humans have no patience at all?

The speaker is a small woman, no taller than Ginny and almost as thin. There are wrinkles around her lips, the telltale sign of a smoker. She holds out a debit card. "I can pay."

"Why?" I can't think of anything else to say.

"I know what it's like. I've been in this situation, or as near as. Card declined, account empty. It's awful, to have to leave it all in the trolley and go home empty-handed. Someone once paid for my shopping, and I'm passing it on. One good deed."

Stunned, I step aside to give her access to the card machine. "Thanks."

"You're welcome."

At the packing shelf, I ask Catherine, "Why did she do that?"

She sighs. "I know you don't believe it, Harry, but most people are nice. They want to help each other. Lately you've been determined to see the worst in everyone."

Outside, the car park is even busier now than it was when we arrived. Growling 4x4s stalk shoppers to their vehicles and hover until the space is vacated, belching diesel fumes. The usual crowd of homeless people clusters around the trolley park, hoping to guilt shoppers into handing over their pound coins.

"Please?" The woman is grey-haired, her cheeks sunken.

One good deed. Why not? I hand over the coin.

She thanks me effusively. I smile, waiting for a flush of pride to fill me up. But as I walk to the car, I feel only foolish. I have given away money and reaped no benefit in return.

Still, perhaps walking away without giving anything would have felt even worse.

In the car, Catherine and Ginny are already waiting, seatbelts fastened. "Come on, Dad," Ginny says. "I want to go home. The football's on TV soon."

Let them wait a moment. There's something I need to figure out.

"What did you mean?" I ask Catherine. "About me seeing the worst in everyone?"

Ginny groans. Catherine sighs. I take the key back out of the ignition.

Finally, Catherine says, "You haven't been yourself lately. I don't think you realise, but it affects everyone around you."

"How?"

"You've been so cold. People have noticed; it's not just me." She lays a hand on my arm. "It's not your fault. The depression is back again, isn't it?"

"Depression?"

"It makes it hard for you to see the good in people."

Dr. Bennington has a condition that affects his ability to observe people? If true, that would invalidate all my research. My time on Earth has seemed unrelentingly negative. For other species, I've been able to see through their flaws and report their virtues fairly.

"Harry, I think you should go back to the doctor."

Something strange is happening to my eyes. They feel hot and itchy. My cheeks are wet.

From the back seat, Ginny says, "I'm sorry, Dad."

My eyes are leaking so much I can't see. Catherine puts her arms around me. She takes the keys from my hand. "Don't worry," she says. "We'll fix this."

Catherine drives us home. I sit in the passenger seat, watching the human world roll by. To me, they still look ugly, angry, and mean. But what if I'm wrong? What if Dr. Bennington's condition has clouded my judgement?

One thing is for sure: I can't leave Earth tomorrow. Let's see what this doctor has to say.

Reaping Rewards

Claire McAneny

Claire McAneny lives and works in rural Ireland. She has always loved stories. Reading them, watching them, listening to them. So, writing stories was a natural progression. You can find Claire on Instagram https://www.instagram.com/ claires.writing.desk/ and via her website clairemcaneny.com where she blogs about writing.

It was a wet Tuesday morning when the taxi pulled up outside. A girl got out, long dark hair reaching down to a skinny waist. Nicola wasn't expecting anyone, but she wasn't so busy she couldn't tell the girl's fortune. Especially if she paid for a taxi to take her all the way out. She didn't look familiar, so Nicola supposed she had come from further away than Rathgormack, the local village.

The doorbell rang and Nicola opened the door. She found it unnerved people too much if they thought she had been watching them from upstairs.

"Are you Nicola Walsh?" the girl asked, standing back from the door.

"I am. You're looking for me?" Nicola kept her voice upbeat and her face as friendly as possible. The girl chewed on her bottom lip as she nodded. Her hair rustled when her head moved.

"Come in," Nicola said, standing back and waving her in. "Do you drink tea? I have some made."

Without waiting for an answer she walked to the kitchen and pulled a chair out from the table.

"I don't mean to interrupt."

"You're grand. I was just about to have tea myself anyway. It's nice to have some company."

The girl sat on the edge of the chair. Nicola moved around the kitchen, rattling cups and crinkling biscuit wrappers. Tom came in looking for a hand out and a pet.

"There you are," Nicola said to him. "As soon as there's biscuits going you appear. Do you have any cats yourself?" she asked the girl.

The girl shook her head but smiled down at Tom when he rubbed against her leg. Tom put on his nicest purr and was eventually rewarded with a gentle head rub. By the time Nicola sat down with the teapot the girl had relaxed a little, and Tom was happy to sit in his bed by the Stanley.

"I'll wait for the tea to settle a little before pouring," Nicola said. "You got a taxi out."

"He's me mam's neighbour. I didn't know where you were and he said he did so he drove me out."

"Sounds like a good neighbour."

"Yea, he used to bring us for spins down the town when we were little."

"Sorry, what's your name?"

"Oh, yea. Kelly, it's Kelly."

"Hi Kelly, nice to meet you."

"I should have said that earlier. Sorry."

Nicola poured the tea and pushed the biscuits towards Kelly after taking one for herself. The thaw had started and Nicola didn't want to scare her away with formality. "How can I help you Kelly?"

Kelly swallowed the bite of the biscuit she had taken. "Mrs. Quinlan in the herbal shop in town gave me your name. She said you'd be able to help me."

Nicola tried to keep the uneasiness from showing on her face. Kelly must want something more than just a love spell.

"I want to get rid of somebody."

Nicola waited to see if she would add anything else. Banishment was not a simple spell.

"Not kill him or anything. Just gone. Away. Somewhere else other than here." Her bottom lip started to shake and she tightened her hold on the cup. Nicola turned away to get the box of tissues. When she turned back Kelly was using her fingers to dab at her eyes. She took a tissue gratefully.

"Sorry, I didn't mean to get upset."

"It means a lot to you," Nicola said and Kelly nodded.

"It's my son's father. He's back from Limerick prison and doing drugs. Not hash or anything. Heroin. And that's his business. We're not together anymore and he's accepted that. He can do what he wants with his life. It's his life," Kelly paused for breath and to stop the mascara filled tears from rolling down her cheeks. "But the other day, he collected Jack from school. He's allowed. He's the father. It's his name on the birth cert and all. He got picked up by the Guards. I had to go down to the station to get him. He had a needle and gear in his pockets."

"Your son's father?"

"Jack. Jack had the gear in his pockets. Slatts had gave it him so the Guards wouldn't find it."

Fresh tears rolled down Kelly's face. Nicola handed her another tissue.

"Did you tell the Guards?"

Kelly shook her head frantically.

"No. He'd kill me. I hid it. He doesn't know I have it yet. But he'll come looking for it."

"You want Slatts out of your life?"

Kelly nodded, her hands squeezing the tissues against the cup.

"Have you thought about moving away?"

"To where? He'd follow us. Jack loves his school. All his friends are here. I don't have the money to go anywhere else." The often repeated phrases spilled out of her lips.

Nicola looked out of the kitchen window. The Comeragh Mountains were hidden by mist and raindrops were dripping off the daffodils in the garden.

"You want your son's father out of your life?" Nicola asked again.

"Or just to forget about him. If he didn't care he'd leave us alone."

"I need to think about it."

Kelly's shoulders slumped as her eyes dropped to the floor. Nicola felt a heart string twang.

"There's a lot involved and it's not something I do regularly. I need to look into it a bit more."

"I have some money and me mam says she can give me some more," Kelly said.

"It's not the money. The spell would need to be done properly for it to be effective. And even then they don't always work. You would need to be part of it too."

Kelly nodded lifting her head to look at Nicola. "I'll do it. Whatever it is, I'll do it."

"I'll look into it and let you know."

"Thanks," Kelly said.

***

Nicola stood on Kelly's doorstep and listened to the chimes of the doorbell fading away. They were replaced by Kelly's footsteps as she walked towards the door. Her face lit up with a smile when she saw Nicola.

"Hi, come in."

She directed Nicola into the small sitting room overflowing with toys.

"I'll get the tea."

Nicola looked around the room. The picture above the fireplace was of Kelly in her pink debs dress with a baby in her arms. He was wearing a suit with a matching pink cravat. She was smiling down at him as he was reaching up for one of the curls of hair loosely arranged on her head.

Kelly returned with two cups and handed one to Nicola. They sat down on the two seater couch opposite the fireplace and television.

"That's a lovely photograph."

"Me mam picked that one. I was thinking of framing another one but it was me mam paying for it."

"That's Jack?"

"Yea, the dressmaker made the tie with the same material as my dress. I was so afraid the suit wouldn't fit him. He grows so fast."

"How old was he there?"

"Eleven months. I had to feed him just before we got the photos took. It was the only way to keep him happy."

"You don't look like you just had a baby."

"I went walking every day with Jack in the buggy. I made sure I lost the weight in time for the debs."

"And what do you do with yourself now when Jack is in school."

"I'll call over to me mam's most days and keep her company."

"Have you thought of doing a course or anything?"

Kelly shook her head. "Nah, not really. I was never any good at school. I could never sit still for long enough. I was always getting shouted at."

Nicola left it and put the cup of tea down on the floor beside her. "I have been doing some looking around and I have worked out how to create the spells."

Kelly held herself very still as she waited for Nicola to continue.

"What you're looking for is not easy. Banishing someone is not straightforward. I can do part of it on my own but I will need you to help me with the rest."

"I'll do it. Whatever it takes. Me mam said she can loan me the money."

"It's not money, Kelly," Nicola paused before she went on. "You'll need to cut your hair."

Kelly said nothing. Her fingers twisted around the lengths of hair spilling over her shoulders.

"Hair holds onto emotions. Cutting the hair will get rid of those old emotions and associations. We'll use it for the knot spell."

"All of it?" Kelly said.

"Yes. All of it."

"Mam, mam, look what I got."

Kelly turned round as Jack burst in the front door waving a toy gun. "A gun. Jack you have loads of toys."

"Seán got it for me."

"He can never have enough toys." Seán Slattery said as he crowded into the sitting room. He filled the doorway as he looked down at them.

"I told you, he doesn't need anything."

"He's a boy. He should be playing with guns. Stop fussing." He said, bemused by Kelly's concern.

Jack started to hit the toy gun against the door frame.

"Mind the door Jack, you'll dent it."

"He's only playing. Don't be at him."

Seán Slattery smiled at Nicola, taking her in with a glance.

Nicola stood up. "I'll head off Kelly. I'll talk to you later."

"Don't leave 'cos of me," Seán said as she passed him.

***

The bright midday sun was shining through the window of Kelly's sitting room. Dust motes danced in the sunbeams as Nicola placed four candles on the floor in front of Kelly. Black for banishment, red for fast action, white for protection, and green for healing.

Nicola repeated a calming mantra to help her focus and concentrated on keeping her breathing steady.

"Calm and still. Still and calm."

She changed to a fire mantra as she lit the wick of the first candle.

"Spark the ember. Kindle the flame."

When she had all four candles lit she looked up and saw the shocked look on Kelly's face. Then she realized she had forgotten to use a match. Full of the magical energy that was flowing through her, Nicola started the first spell before Kelly could change her mind. She handed her a black permanent marker.

"Draw an X on the photograph of Seán and say the lines on the sheet with me as you hold the photograph in the flame."

Kelly drew a slightly wobbly X over her ex boyfriend's face. The flame from the black candle flickered greedily around the photo as she joined in with Nicola.

"Oh Mighty Goddess Nemesis,

Bring Seán Paul Slattery to justice.

Let him receive his just rewards.

What goes out comes back three times three.

This is my will, so let it be."

Kelly dropped the last fragment into the bright flame before it burned her fingers. There was a strong smell from the basil and frankincense oil that Nicola had anointed the candle with.

For the second spell Nicola handed Kelly large metal scissors. Kelly slowly reached out her hand to take them. Her shoulders rose and fell as she took a deep breath. Then she took one of the many small plaits in her hair and cut it close to her scalp. Nicola nodded and smiled at her.

"You're doing fine. Now think about what you want to change as you tie a knot and then hold it over the black candle."

Kelly stared at the plait in her hand and then tied it in a tight knot. Once again, there was an aroma of basil and frankincense as the flames from the black candle began to consume Kelly's knotted hair. The intense smell of burning hair mixed with the smell from the black candle.

"This is what was, not what will be. This is what was, not what will be."

Kelly's firm voice joined in with Nicola's calm recitation. Her voice became louder as she fed her plaited hair to the flame of the black candle. There was a loud sizzle as the flame rose up to take the end of the plait.

Kelly's hands moved quickly to cut the next plait and tie a knot. But before she could burn it in the black candle Nicola moved her hand to the red candle beside it.

"This is for fast action, for quick results. This is for fast action, for quick results."

Kelly paused as she listened to the words Nicola was chanting. She joined in as the second plait sizzled in the flame from the candle.

Following the sequence Kelly held the third plait over the next candle, the white one. Nicola nodded and started to speak again.

"This is for protection, to prevent harm. This is for protection, to prevent harm."

When the flames from the green candle began to melt Kelly's hair the smell of eucalyptus and rosemary filled the room.

"This is to heal the soul and protect the spirit. This is to heal the soul and protect the spirit."

Kelly repeated the action with each of the candles until all of her plaits were gone. The hair on her head stood up and stuck out at odd angles. The smoke from the candles filled the sitting room. It curled and spun lazily in the warm sunlight.

Kelly stared at the flames dancing on the candles as Nicola lit the oil burner on the mantelpiece. Soon, the healing smells of rosemary and sandalwood mingled with the other smells in the room.

"That's the hard part done now Kelly. I'll tidy up down here while you have a shower."

* * *

When Jack came home from school, he was greeted by a large white page, two paintbrushes and two pots of paint. For the third spell, Kelly and Jack worked together to paint a picture to hang on the wall of Jack's bedroom. The page was soon filled with peaceful blues and soothing greens. Kelly's small, careful strokes and Jack's larger, more exuberant ones. A few of his strokes continued onto the wooden floor which made Nicola smile. She had mixed the paint carefully, filling it with positive affirmations and good intentions.

Kelly's newly cut hair bounced as the two heads bent together. It tickled Jack's ear and he giggled loudly. Kelly had washed and dried it and attempted to style it. She hadn't said anything but Nicola had seen her checking her reflection in the mirror. Her fingers continually tried to tuck the too short strands behind her ear.

***

"...The Gardaí arrested a local man who was remanded in custody to Limerick prison. Seán Slattery with an address at Ballylynch, Carrick on Suir will await trial for possession with intent to supply. Judge Hartnett refused bail based on previous convictions for possession and assault. If sentenced Mr. Slattery is facing ten years imprisonment. That's all from the newsroom here at WLR fm. Back to the studio."

Maiasaura Deifaeria

Jennifer Lee Rossman

Jennifer Lee Rossman (any pronouns) is a queer, disabled, and autistic author and editor from Binghamton, New York. Follow them on Twitter @JenLRossman and find more of their work at http://jenniferleerossman.blogspot.com

There's an old proverb we godparents like to quote: do not wish on shooting stars, for they are meteors and you are dinosaurs.

What? I did say it was an *old* proverb. One of the oldest, not counting that one about giving a fish a leg and he eats for a day, but teach a fish to grow a leg and he eats on land for the rest of his life, but we aren't encouraged to meddle with evolution anymore, so we don't get to use that one as often.

But back to the dinosaur proverb. It's a Memento Mori. A reminder that death is inevitable. Death finds a way.

No matter how much you wish, you can't stop a meteor from carving out the Chicxulub crater like a melon baller and wiping out the world as you know it. Everything will not be okay just because you believe it will be, and there's nothing you can do in the grand scheme of things.

I know, I know. Depressing as heck. But it's not like you modern humans are so cheerful in the metaphor department, with your multiple methods of cat skinning and needing to remind people not to discard children with bathwater...

For millions of years, I would warn the little hatchlings I protected, try to prepare them in case they were the last generation. Oh yes, I have many powers, my dear, but even I can't see the future. I could only tell them with certainty that extinction came for everyone.

I would help them with the smaller wishes in life, opportunities to find mates and feeding grounds, the occasional transformation of an allosaur into a stegosaur, that sort of thing. All the while, reminding them not to waste what precious little time they had wishing on extinction disguised as streaking lights in the sky.

In the end, when it finally happened, I found myself wishing someone had warned *me* how much I would miss them.

***

Sixty-five million years. That's how long I grieved.

Alone. On the edges of existence. Waiting. For what, I have no idea. It wasn't as if they were ever coming back.

In retrospect, I could have moved on. Evolved into a fairy godmother for birds like the rest of them.

But dinosaurs had been my darlings for so long, longer than they had been gone. You don't just move on from three geological periods of dedication and love that quickly.

I don't even know if moving on after that is possible. They were the loves of my life, every single one of them from the first plateosaur I took care of when I was a bumbling newbie to the last little triceratops who didn't have time to get her wish granted before the universe violently thrust us into the Cenozoic without regard for our opinions on the matter.

That kind of love forms a connection that can never be broken. Once a godmother, always a godmother, and I knew when my godhatchlings needed me.

Even after 65 million years, even after her bones had mineralized.

She needed me.

***

Earth had moved on, even if I hadn't.

In the absence of dinosaurs, Time had redecorated, drying up our shallow sea and the valleys where we frolicked. All right, I didn't do much frolicking. Not much of a frolicker. But I was frolicking adjacent.

I probably shouldn't have been surprised at the changes. In my time as a godmother, I had seen the Triassic become the Jurassic become the Cretaceous, seen continents move and mountains form, seen grasses evolve into trees.

But I was *part* of that.

This...all of this happened without my knowledge or consent, the landscape turned to rocky desert populated by birds and little lizards and those peculiar fuzzy creatures that gave birth without eggs and fed their young with a white liquid produced from their breasts.

Mammals. Oh, mammals. Baffling things that had never been much of an evolutionary factor in my time, but my tyrant lizard kings had left an empty throne, and somehow, mammals had seized it.

In a distant way, I could sense the change in the air. Pollution. Noise. Chaos. Not overly harmful, but it was beginning.

Angry, unfamiliar vocalizations carried on the wind, in the same direction that I felt the pull of my last godhatchling. I hurried over a hill and found two groups of bipedal mammals shouting, performing what I can only describe as threat displays.

These were the animals destiny and chance chose to replace the dinosaurs?

But I couldn't ponder on that for long; my attention was drawn to a huge, ugly gouge in the earth. A wound, perhaps, would be the better word.

And protruding from that wound, a fossilized dinosaur skull.

I swear, I felt the meteor hit a second time because I would know that face anywhere.

***

The mammals–humans, basically a specialized sort of primate too smart for their own good–stopped their fight immediately upon seeing me. Most froze in place, several let out terrified screams and ran for the tents, and one fainted outright.

Now perhaps I should have altered my appearance, as I did once upon another era, making myself resemble the species I was showing myself to. Perhaps nothing in their lives could have prepared them for the sight of an iridescent white and pink, 30 foot long triceratops fairy hovering over the landscape on dragonfly wings.

Well, nothing in my life had prepared me for the sight of a bunch of overgrown lemurs desecrating the final resting place of my Asha, so the feeling was mutual.

I glared at them, analyzing the social hierarchy. They were of two separate packs, that much was clear, but none of them had the aura of an alpha. Where were the matriarchs?

Something struck my foot. I turned slowly. A rock.

I locked eyes with the one foolish enough to throw a rock at me, and I may have resembled a herbivore, but I outweighed them 400 to 1 and my face was made for stabbing, with three horns that were half the length of their puny human bodies. I was, in a word, imposing.

And that was before I used my magic to bridge the communication barrier between us and speak to them in their language, my voice low and rumbling like a distant herd of stampeding brontosaurs.

"Get me your alphas." For a moment, no one moved. I took heavy, snorting breaths, waiting. Then I added, in a voice that left no room for debate, "*Now.*"

As they ran, I gave a shake of my nose horn, the magic one with the little star on the end, casting a spell that would make them forget my appearance after they did as I asked. Then I sank to the ground, my rage leaving me for the moment, and went to nuzzle the earthly remains of my girl.

***

Had I known Asha would be my last, I would have done things differently. I would have granted her wish personally, let myself be the family she wanted. Needed.

She was an orphan. The only survivor of a nest raid, her parents having been driven out of the breeding ground never knowing one egg had been left behind to hatch in a lonely world.

She had one wish: to be loved.

Now, love is a tricky thing, even for fairies. You can't make someone love anyone, you can only bring them together and hope.

"*You* love me," she said one day after another herd declined to adopt her as their own. "Why can't I just be yours?"

"I do love you. I love all of my hatchlings. But one day, we will both move on. I will need to help another hatchling, and you will grow up and have your own family." I gave her adolescent neck frill a gentle nudge. "Now come, my dear. Let's keep looking."

***

At the sound of approaching footsteps, I raised my head from the fossil to see one of the alphas. Supposedly, anyway. In my day, pack leaders tended to be the most physically fit, agile specimens. And female.

Standing before me was a scrawny, pale thing with ridiculous whiskers that looked like an evolutionary holdover from when humans lived underground like moles. He introduced himself as Edward Drinker Cope, and he didn't scream or faint or throw rocks at me because I decided being a triceratops fairy was not conducive to positive communication with the humans.

I hoped I made a good human. Accurate, if nothing else. I had made my hair longer than the male's, my face more becoming, on a hunch that if any gender in this species was the flashier and more attractive one it could not possibly be the male.

And anyway, I had always wanted long eyelashes.

"Can I help you?" he said, more of a tired statement than a proper question, as if I had interrupted something important that he would rather be doing.

I faltered. Could he help me? I honestly didn't even know what I wanted. He couldn't bring her back, couldn't give her the love

I could have given her if I hadn't been so preoccupied with whether I should.

I looked down at my gangly primate hands, at a loss. I think I wanted to blame him. Punish him because I couldn't punish the meteor but still needed someone to be mad at after all this time. But there wasn't really anything—

There was a strange choking sound. I glanced up. Edward Drinker Cope had finally acknowledged the existence of my wings, and no longer cared whether or not he could help me.

He fell to his knees, hands clasped together. "Oh, angel of the Lord, I thank you for blessing me with thy divine presence."

I lowered the bushy bits above my eyes in confusion. "I beg your pardon, primate? What did you call me?"

"Are you not an angel? Sent by the Lord to bless my excavation and lay waste to that of my rival?"

"Noooo," I said slowly, very slowly, drawing out the word while I tried to parse what he was talking about. "Tell me of this rivalry?"

He told me that he and the other alpha, Marsh, had been friends, but petty feuds had turned into a great war to discover the most species of dinosaurs. At first I thought war a strong word, but he went on to describe sabotage and physical altercations and...

"...and sometimes, if a site has been good to us and we do not want it to fall into their hands, we dynamite the rest."

I stood very still, anger and revulsion broiling inside me. "Dynamite," I whispered, prompting the man to provide me with a definition of this unfamiliar word that made me uneasy with dread.

"We destroy it," Cope elaborated. "We get one skeleton, and we destroy the rest so they can't get them."

This was my first time having hands, and I found that I quite liked the way they felt curled into fists.

I was silent for a good, long while, seething. I don't know precisely how long. Anything less than 65 million years may as well have been an instant.

I had to stop him. Not just for Asha, but for everyone. And that is why I forced my fingers to relax, turned the corners of my lips upward while being careful not to bare my teeth, and spoke with the same motherly voice I had used when introducing myself to all of my godhatchlings.

"No, my sweet little evolved ape. I'm afraid I am not this angel of the Lord creature of which you speak."

Utter devastation came over Cope's face.

"Oh, but don't despair, my dear, for I am something even better" —And here I spread my arms and wings for maximum drama— "I am your fairy godmother."

***

Death is a part of life. Always has been, always will be. That's why you don't waste time wishing on shooting stars.

Asha knew that better than most, having come into this world alone and surrounded by shattered egg shells. But she was a herbivore; she didn't require death to live like the carnivores, and to say the concept of predation bothered her would be an understatement on par with saying continental drift was not the quickest method of travel.

We came across a carcass one day, a small hadrosaur that had been picked nearly clean. Asha pressed into my flank as we walked, though the kill was not fresh and the predator could be miles away.

I stopped, gently nodded toward the skeleton. "Bones are not for sadness. They are not for grieving. They just *are*."

"It was someone," she said quietly.

"It was. And now it is not, and it is sad that their transition from *being* to *having been* needed to happen, but they are not in those bones any more than they were in the meat on them. The instant the life left, it stopped being some*one* and started being some*thing*."

She twitched her tail in frustration. "But. But they were here. Someone loved them. How could they just leave the bones for scavengers? It's not..."

"Dignified?" I asked. "No, it certainly isn't. But the bones don't care. So neither should we."

***

It wasn't dignified. Disturbing her final resting place, ripping her from the earth just to win some asinine feud.

"I would like you to explain the purpose of all this," I said quietly to Cope as we watched his men brush dust away from Asha. Much as I wanted to stop it, to magic away their tools and send a sandstorm to tuck her back to sleep, this was more than simply the pastime of a man with more resources than good sense. The way he spoke...he made it sound like this was common. Like people made a habit of digging for bones.

"I told you," he grumbled. "I need to find more than he does, that no-good Darwinian know-it-all. Grant my wish, make it so he can never find a fossil again."

He was nicer when he thought me an angel of the Lord.

"And I told *you*," I reminded him, squinting in the bright sunlight, "magic is not as simple as that. I need to understand what it is, why it is." I gestured to the dig. "Why does it matter what you do with her after?"

"It's paleontology. We study them. Put them on display in museums. And there's great honor in being the one who finds the most new ones."

Down the hill, someone found a tibia. My own words echoed in my ear from long ago. So did Asha's.

She was not in those bones any more now than she had been before Time meticulously replaced every cell with mineral. It was just fossils. A skeleton. It wasn't her.

But it had been once.

They had all been someone.

"Mr. Cope," I said, because I had a feeling that "you strange little egotistical monkey in a suit" was not the preferred way to refer to people. "I will indeed grant your wish, but first I must speak to your rival."

***

Her horns were growing longer, curving; I found I didn't have to lean down so far to nudge her shoulder anymore. Almost overnight, she had entered a new era of life. Adolescence.

And still, she was with me.

Was her wish really so difficult to grant? Had I lost my touch?

"Do predators feel?"

I blinked at her sudden question. "What do you mean, dear?"

She tilted her head this way and that, thinking, watching the shadow of her growing frill on the grass. "Are they like us, god-mother? Do they have thoughts and feelings? Do they love?"

"Yes." Of all the questions she had asked in her life, this was the easiest to answer. I'd been the godmother to uncountable preda-tors in my time, each of them exactly as vulnerable and sweet and loving as Asha.

"But they kill."

"They do. That's how they were made, that's how they work. It isn't a choice."

I paused, fondly remembering one little allosaur so distraught over the thought of being a predator that she wished for me to transform her into a stegosaur. And I did, only to turn her back after a day and a half when she desperately missed her family.

Granting her wish had more to do with helping her come to terms with the way things are and less to do with actual magic, but that's the way it is sometimes.

***

To his credit, Othniel Charles Marsh, the alpha male of the rival pack, was larger and more imposing than Cope. Fascinating whiskers, as well. But that is the extent of the good things I can say about him.

He was just like Cope. Greedy, petty, having no regard for the sanctity of the bones he pried from the rocks and blasted into nonexistence for the sake of making himself feel less inferior.

He did not call me an angel of the Lord, but his wish was the same as the other horrid mammal.

"Help me beat him, I beg of you. His scientific ideas go against every rational thought! It infuriates me that his may well be the victorious side. I've heard he recently found a triceratops specimen. They moved in herds, you know, probably a whole family of them where that one came from."

There was not.

"But he's going to blast the site so I can't find the rest. You know what I should do?"

I opened my mouth to say, "Retire from paleontology and return to the subterranean lifestyle from which your long touch-receptor-like whiskers likely evolved?" but he did not pause long enough for me to answer.

"I should dynamite his dig tonight!"

And with that, he confirmed for me that there was no good side in this war. There were only two predators, heartless men who had made a choice to cheat and destroy and hate. And for no reason at all.

I wanted to believe this was just the way of things. That the dinosaurs died and it was sad, heartbreakingly devastating, but that good could come from it if it helped humans learn about the world and their place in it. That maybe they would realize they were also dinosaurs, and stop wishing on shooting stars.

But they didn't care about any of that. They just wanted to win. They wanted to enjoy destroying history, graves.

Before I talked to Marsh, before I talked to Cope, I thought it was just Asha in trouble. It wasn't, but there was little I could do about that unless I brought about the end of paleontology. Not that I would be able to; I was still Asha's godmother, and any magic had to be in service of her wish, not mine.

Before I talked to the rival humans, I thought perhaps I could convince them to stop the digs, but I was wrong about that, too.

I needed to refine my focus.

Asha. *She* was my godhatchling, not the rest of them. It was her I needed to protect, even if I couldn't do it way back when.

***

Asha was on the cusp of sexual maturity, complete with all the angst and emotional upheaval I was not equipped to help her with.

I had raised her to adulthood somehow, not just as a godmother but as a *mother*. And not a good one, apparently.

"You said it couldn't be you," she roared, her voice bellowing in the lower frequencies. "You said I would find someone who would love me, because we would both have to move on one day so it couldn't be you." She reared up on her hind legs and slammed her front feet on the dirt. "But have you noticed, godmother? It was you. And if you had just let it be you from the beginning, let yourself love me completely–"

I snorted and made a mock charge toward her, my wings buzzing in a fury. "Do not," I warned. "Do not suggest that I gave you anything less than my full–"

She didn't flinch at my charge. "But you didn't. You were so afraid of losing me, you wouldn't let yourself." She threw her head back in defiance, her frill and horns striking a powerful silhouette against the sunset orange sky. "I know this is true, because if I was really loved as much as I wished for, you would have had to move on and be someone else's godmother."

And with that, she stormed off.

I decided we both needed some alone time, and didn't go after her.

Some alone time. *Some*, dammit. Not 65 million years.

***

I couldn't have saved Asha then. It was a meteor and she was a dinosaur and no amount of wishing on a shooting star could change that.

But she was right. I hadn't moved on because I couldn't, not until I granted her wish, not until I did right by her.

I will admit, I didn't know the first thing about dynamite. Only that Othniel Charles Marsh intended to use it on the dig site where her remains lay, and that it was dangerous.

That was all I *needed* to know.

"I did love you," I told her, resting my chin on the ground beside her half-exposed skeleton. "As much as I could have. And it breaks my heart that it wasn't enough for you, it wasn't what you deserved."

I fluttered my wings and twitched my tail; that always made her laugh.

"I hope tonight changes that. I hope it shows you how far I would go for you, how loved you were and still are."

Just a little magic, and the dynamite would be useless. Both camps' stash. And while they blamed each other of sabotage, I would wrap Asha in a blanket of sand, hide her away from the greedy humans.

I felt that pull again, our connection. But it wasn't her needing me this time.

This wasn't a solution and I knew it. The humans would blame each other, the war would escalate. That was no way to show my love, no way to grant her wish and move on. And I needed to move on.

***

She was still in the nest when I found her. Tiny thing, lost and alone and helpless.

She looked up at me with those giant eyes full of hope as I landed beside her. I think mine was the first friendly face she had ever seen.

"Hello, my dear," I said gently. "I am your fairy godmother."

She just stared at me.

"That means I'm here to help you. Make a wish, and I will make it come true."

The little hatchling wasted no time. "I want love."

"Love," I repeated. "Well, there's all different kinds of love, and all different things that we mean when we say the word. What is love to you?"

This question took some thought, but finally she had an answer. "Love is when everyone around you is happy because you exist, and their lives are better because you are in it. And. And...it's forever. It's in your bones."

***

She was the star attraction of the museum. A perfectly preserved and intact subadult triceratops.

The men who found her, insignificant men whose names would soon be lost to history, had been embroiled in a vicious rivalry. Indeed, one of the groups had been intending to destroy her partially excavated skeleton in order to sabotage his enemy.

So imagine his surprise when he found her completely uncovered, as if the wind had done all the hard work, her bones arranged in such a way as to suggest she died striking a defiant pose, head held high and ready to fight some unknown predator. How could he possibly destroy something so beautiful? Even his rival agreed, and they took joint credit in her discovery.

She inspired everyone who saw her. She made them happy.

They loved her, forever, deep down to the bone.

I suppose I was right. No matter how much I loved her, she couldn't be mine. She was everybody's.

As I turned to leave the museum, I felt that pull.

But it wasn't Asha this time. It was a little human girl. And it was time for me to move on.

Daemonum Ex

Hannah Hulbert

Hannah Hulbert is an author from the south coast of England. She has two children, a husband and an affinity for goblin culture.

Everelda lifted her gas lamp to illuminate the dripping, russet curve of the sewer ceiling. The flame guttered and flared, burning blue on the billowing miasma. She splashed on through the trickle of putrid water running down the centre, disregarding the foulness splattering over her tall hunting boots. The sewers had been built a mere ten years ago and already the stench had embedded itself into the walls. She tried to imagine being reduced to living in these conditions, before reminding herself that she owed these beings nothing. She was here on a mission to bind one, not to empathise.

At last she reached the junction. The nest lay beyond the northern entrance, if her earlier divinations were accurate. Of course, hunting the creature down would've been considerably easier had Lord Fortesque deigned to divulge the demon's name. But Everelda was no novice. The vaulted chamber had that familiar atmosphere she had come to recognise, of darkness deeper than mere shadows. This was the spot.

At least the ground here was clear. She set down the lamp, took out a chalk, and began drawing a circle on the mercifully dry ground.

It was an incomplete circle: an open trap, with the gap parallel to the north passage's gaping mouth. Around the perimeter of the completed section, she painstakingly copied out the words to the Lord's Prayer in Latin, gut twisting at the blasphemy. Gone were the days when she could draw upon her own dark powers —her respectable clients would never stand for that. Instead, she confined herself to the guild-approved methods. She bit her lip, trailing behind her words of borrowed power, too great for even a demon to pass through once activated.

Task complete and chalk still clutched in her palm, Everelda slipped her hand into her waistcoat pocket. The cold, smooth cylinder under her fingertips reassured her that everything was going according to plan. And so she baited the trap -with herself.

And not a moment too soon.

A towering column of darkness separated out from the black of the north passage, sniffing out her feeble soul. The demon bristled with talons and horns, swayed with the lashing of a serpentine tail, fluttered with the spreading of vast, leathery wings. Its claws clicked against the bricks underfoot as it stalked closer, gleaming like oil on water in the undulating light.

Everelda felt her legs weaken as it approached. She recognised that form, that musk, that deep, purring rumble. Her chest tightened, as though all the air was being squeezed from her lungs. It couldn't be...But it was.

"Everelda," spoke the voice of the abyss as they stepped into the pool of lamplight, joining her inside the circle. They hadn't noticed the chalk on the ground, but they weren't the only one here caught off guard. "Of all the sewers in all the world, for you to arrive in mine."

"Marthim," Everelda replied, her voice faltering. This was the demon Lord Fortesque had sent her to bind? What was she to do, so woefully unprepared? Her mind raced between working out how she could still fulfil her contract and how she could weasel out of it.

She wasn't ready for this. She was a mess. She ran her fingertips through her straggly hair, wishing she'd dragged a comb through it that morning. After years of imagining what would happen if she saw them again, imagining what she would say and how suave she would act, she found herself at a loss. She clenched the chalk in the hand behind her back as her carefully laid plans crumbled around her.

Marthim planted their taloned hands on their hips and cast an appraising glance across her person, lingering on her grubby trousers. She shivered as they absorbed every inch of her, drinking her in. She had forgotten how they could do that. Oh, Lord, the ecstasy of being known so utterly. Thank goodness they could not read her mind. If they knew what she was planning...

"You're looking well," the demon continued.

Everelda waved her empty hand as if to bat away the compliment. "No, I don't. You, however..." She floundered, for they were more resplendent in power and sinister beauty than she had remembered. And she had remembered often over the years. Her pulse quickened. A small voice at the back of her mind reminded her that she had a job to do, but it was almost impossible to hear over the blood pounding through her temples.

"I do try, but it's so hard when one is reduced to living in a sewer." They preened a little, arching their slender neck. "So. I hear you've turned Hunter these days?"

Straight to the point, just as they had always been.

"That's right," Everelda replied. She took a cautious step to one side, hoping to appear nonchalant. "Got to pay the bills some-how. And I've got the knack, apparently."

The pungent air quivered with laughter. "That's one way of putting it," Marthim said. "You certainly captured my heart, oh cruel master. And now you unleash your fury at my abandon-ment of you upon the rest of my kind?"

Everelda's insides squirmed. How could they possibly know how it felt, to go from being connected to a power so immense and invasive to being suddenly alone? How could she articulate the void in her being that they had left? Fury was so small a part of her maelstrom of emotion. When they had left, they had taken everything that brought meaning to her world, including her enthusiasm for the occult. Hunting was the only solace she had managed to find, some small connection that tethered her to their world. How could she even begin to explain? The rift between them was too great.

No. There would be no explanations. She was here to perform a duty. She continued to move herself in tiny increments around the inside of the circle. Marthim turned slowly with her, match-ing step for step, moving away from the gap on the northern sec-tion of the trap. Their body swayed like a mesmerising cobra as they followed her lead.

"You don't mean that," Everelda found herself saying. "We were both to blame for what happened."

The column of shade shrugged. "Maybe. Or maybe it was nei-ther. We were different entities back then. Let's not regress."

Everelda had reached a quarter of the way around the circle and dwindled to a fraction of her resolve. Marthim tilted their head, awaiting her response, tail swishing gracefully behind, almost invisible in the shadows.

"You're right, let's let bygones be bygones." Her stomach clenched with guilt at what she was about to do.

"So. Are you here in a professional capacity?" Marthim asked.

"You could say that."

"You're here to catch a demon?" they asked, voice bright with interest. "Anyone I know?"

"Could be," Everelda said. Only a few more steps and she would reach the incomplete section and this whole wretched ordeal would be over. Their many glinting eyes fixed on hers, as they danced to the rhythm of the earth's pulse. Sweat beaded on Everelda's brow.

"Not Jezebel, the poor dear? She's had such a time. Or Mephistopheles? You know, he's quite down-and-out these days."

"No, neither of them." One more step and she would be at the gap. The sooner she completed her task and put Marthim behind herself the better. As if she could ever put Marthim behind herself. She hadn't managed to yet. She clutched at the stick of chalk like a talisman.

"Well, then, I fear you may have come to the wrong stretch of the sewers. The only other demon around here is..."

Everelda dropped to the ground, spun around and closed the gap in the circle with one arc of her hand. Her heartbeat thundered through her entire body.

"Me?" said Marthim, voice quavering a little.

"I'm sorry," Everelda whispered, stepping out of the circle, leaving them standing there, alone. Their wings fluttered. "It's not personal. Lord Fortesque hired me when you bailed on your contract."

"Everelda?" Marthim cried with such pathos that Everelda had to turn away as she uttered the words that would make eternal the binding of the Holy Circle. They caught in her throat as she chanted, choking her with her own hypocrisy as she petitioned the Almighty. Then she snatched the vial of holy water from her pocket and smashed it on the ground, showering the words with glass and droplets. She looked up with tear-blurred eyes.

Marthim stood exactly as they had been before, elegantly composed and utterly unbound. Everelda's mouth opened wordlessly of its own volition.

"You of all people should know that only works on a demon already contained within a circle," they chided.

"But you are..." Everelda said, and as she did so her eyes traced her chalk outline.

The stretch that she had manoeuvred Marthim to turn their back to had been deliberately and meticulously erased. She shot a glance at their winding tail. The obsidian scales were pale with chalk dust.

"I was prepared to face any of your wiles, Everelda. In fact, I was quite looking forward to the challenge. I have to say, a single line of chalk was rather a disappointment."

"But how?" she gasped. Marthim took a step forward, so that the long claws on their toes teased over the line.

"...Did I know you were coming?" they finished for her. "That was easy. I used Lord Fortesque, knowing he would hire you when I walked out on him. He actually tried to summon Azazel, can you even imagine? Of course, she didn't show up, so I did instead. Granted a few requests, killed off a couple of his rivals, turned a hay bale into a horse, you know the drill. And then I ran away with a sackful of his family heirlooms, just to make a point." They chuckled and the sound was like the glorious victory cry of a thousand hyenas. "Honestly, why else would I ever enter a contract with someone so dull?"

The memories trickled back from the recesses of Everelda's mind, familiar yet richer with the fermentation of time. They always had been beguiling and infuriating in equal measures. She ran her tongue over her dry lips.

"So...you engineered this meeting? What do you want, Marthim? If you're after vengeance against me after all these years..." Her insides contracted at the thought. The sickening anticipation of agony mingled with the sweet promise of justice. She gazed up at them with wide eyes.

"Oh, please don't be so melodramatic. I just want to talk."

"Talk?" Her mind scrambled for a firm foundation. "If you wanted to talk, why didn't you just come and see me? I'm not exactly hiding and you certainly don't lack the means."

"Turn up in your pokey little room above the fishmonger's in all my glory and wrong-foot you? Make you all defensive? No, no. This way was much better."

That nagging guilt at betraying Marthim: that had all been masterfully engineered. She ought to be outraged, yet she couldn't bring herself to feel anything but...what was this? A brightness?

Hope? No. The best she could hope for now was Lord Fortesque calling down the constabulary upon her head. Everelda sighed.

"Whatever happened between us?" she asked.

"Well, I've been thinking about that a lot recently." They smiled at Everelda's expression of surprise. "You know it's not like me to dwell on a mortal so. Do you know what I concluded? That the time simply wasn't right for us."

Everelda's eyebrows rose.

"You were so young, and hungry for fire. You fell in love with my power as much as anything. And I was proud and unyielding—I make no apologies for that. But you changed, as you began to suspect that there was more to life than witchcraft. Matured. You wanted more, and I was...unwilling to provide it. The differences between us became too great to be spanned by carnal attraction. And then the spark between us died. That's all."

Everelda stared. How could something so tumultuous be so casually summarised? There must be more to it than that. But when Everelda replayed those dusty, painful memories, she could find no flaws in their assessment. They were supernatural, after all.

"Before that, though," Everelda said, her voice tremulous;,eager, "we were..." What was the word? Happy? No, that couldn't be right, it was far too small.

"Yes," Marthim said, their voice soft yet mighty, understanding her unspoken meaning as they always could. They couldn't read her mind, but they knew her so well that it made little difference. "And I believe we could be again." They stepped over the chalk line, overwhelming Everelda with their magnificent presence. "I've missed you."

A weakness seeped into her knees.

"But we changed. We lost the spark. And I said all those things..."

"You changed. We grew apart." They stepped closer again, close enough that their musk almost drowned her. She gulped in deep breaths of them, filling herself. "But then...I changed too. And I think you might've changed again. You're not the same witch who said all those things. I think it might be time to try again, if you want to."

Everelda raised a hand to catch the sob as it bubbled out of her mouth. Marthim offered a fantasy that she'd never dared to entertain. Yet, here they were, separated by nothing but a mere foot of dirty brickwork and nearly two decades of regret. She cleared her throat before venturing to speak.

"But where in the world could we belong -a demon like you and a wretch like me? Lord Fortesque will be after us both in the city; we can't stay here in the sewers; I abandoned the Sisterhood long ago..." It was too good to be true. There was no way this could work out.

"Are you accepting my proposal?" Marthim asked, a curve of fangs flashing in the dark.

"Yes, I am," Everelda said with a heady rush. She didn't even pause to consider. The truth burst out of her, as though it had been held up behind her tongue, waiting to be spoken for half a lifetime. And once the words were out, the weight of them lifted from her shoulders. She beamed up at Marthim.

"Now, where are we going?"

They fanned their wings and drew themselves up to their full, formidable height. Their power throbbed in time to Everelda's pulse. She loosened her stiff collar, suddenly stifling.

"I was hoping you'd permit me to take you to visit my family?" they said in a voice as smooth as a dagger through velvet.

To hell? She baulked, mind reeling.

"Don't worry. They'll adore you." Marthim said, reading the uncertainty on her face. "And we don't have to stay if you don't want to. The whole world is at our feet."

She turned the thought over in her imagination and it dawned on her that this was the perfect place for the pair of them, if they were a pair. She felt giddy at the concept.

"But I'm a Hunter..."

"A witch," Marthim corrected, without a hint of uncertainty. "Once a witch, always a witch."

The final piece of her that had been missing slotted back into place.

"Then I would be honoured," she said with a grin and a stately bow. They clapped their terrible talons together like a gleeful child and her heart almost burst with adoration.

"But first," she amended, and Marthim froze, arching their multitude of eyebrows, "let's pay Lord Fortesque's bedchamber a visit. I did promise to deliver you to him after all."

Marthim's eyes blazed in the dim light of the sewer, and then they burst into peals of terrific laughter.

"I am delighted to see that you have not changed too much," they said. "What a wonderfully wicked idea."

Marthim reached out and, after what seemed an eternity of waiting, brushed their razor-sharp fingertips gently—oh, so gently—down Everelda's tweed jacket sleeves. Their hands closed around hers. She turned her face up to meet the full awe-inspiring wonder of theirs. Then they enfolded her in the most luxurious rolls of darkness, consuming the sewer, their past, the whole of Everelda's mundane reality.

And the demon and the witch winked out of existence, together.

The End of Sleep

Jamie M. Boyd

Jamie M. Boyd is a writer and former
journalist based in Florida.

Dr. Ocan Kato stared at the bill and fought off a wave of bitterness—the compulsion to simultaneously laugh and cry and vomit his breakfast into the kitchen sink.

The bill was from the fertility clinic, the one where his wife's eggs waited, frozen like miniature snowballs. Normally, they charged the annual storage fee to his wife's credit card, but the number needed updating. A representative had called her cell phone, but she never answered.

"Please respond in a timely manner with a new method of payment to ensure your future is not compromised."

Ocan read those mocking words four times. *Future. Compromised.*

He tore the letter in half and chucked the pieces into the garbage, the sweep of his arm knocking his coffee off the counter. As the porcelain shattered on the tile floor, the sound was almost gratifying; the house was always so quiet now.

Hot liquid splattered against his leg, the wall, leaving a dripping, Rorschach stain. He'd hated that wallpaper when she picked it out. All those silly, little blue flowers. But Eimy had liked them, said she wanted their first home to feel comfortable, even kitschy. His jaw worked at the memory.

Slowly, he gathered the pieces of the broken mug, careful not to cut himself on their perfect, curved edges. He sopped up the puddle. Then, with a clean dishtowel, he carefully–meticulously–wiped down the wallpaper.

***

After Dr. Ocan Kato changed his slacks, he called a car.

"Durham VA Medical Center," he instructed as he slipped inside.

As the vehicle drove itself along the highway, Ocan opened his laptop and reviewed the files of the PTSD patients he was scheduled to see that day, throwing their medical records onto the windshield. First up was Capt. Eric Adams, who'd lost most of his Air Force squadron in the war with North Korea. He suffered from violent nightmares and sleep walking. He'd finally sought professional help when he woke to find himself strangling his own wife.

After the car dropped Ocan off at the hospital entrance, he headed to his office on the tenth floor. Although he preferred to dive right into seeing patients like Adams, he had a meeting to endure first.

"Major, welcome," Ocan said as his 9 a.m. appointment arrived.

Major Claire Weissman sported a square jaw, a thick shock of white hair cut blunt to her chin, and a uniformed lackey who filed into the room behind her. Ocan didn't know the purpose of this visit, but when you work at the VA and an Army officer with a PhD in neuroscience wants to speak with you, you listen.

"Dr. Kato, what do you know about unilateral sleep?" she asked as they took their seats.

Ocan hesitated. He hadn't heard that term since comparative biology class.

"Unilateral sleep enables birds and some mammals, like dolphins, to sleep with only half of their brain at a time," he answered carefully. "That's how birds fly across the ocean without stopping. How prey keep an eye open all night for predators."

"Exactly." Weissman nodded. "And it wouldn't be hard to imagine what that ability would mean for humans. The applications, for a solider. A pilot."

"You're not —" He squelched the urge to say the idea was ridiculous and merely frowned. "I'm afraid that's the opposite of what I do, which is try to restore normal, healthy sleep."

"And that's exactly why we're here." She smiled with the indulgence of a woman who held a winning hand. "We've already achieved unisleep in fourteen subjects. I want to talk to you about the unintended side effects."

Ocan gaped. "What...went wrong?" Aside from, oh, *everything*.

"Nothing. In fact, insomnia and other psychological issues improved. We want you to do a bigger study. We may have stumbled onto a cure for PTSD." She nodded to the young man beside her. "Meet Sgt. Joseph Valdoni, our first successful unisleep patient."

Ocan re-evaluated the solider to her right.

"Six months and counting, sir," the young man said with a serious nod. "In fact, I'm half-sleeping right now."

Holy hell. Ocan turned to Weissman. "Impossible."

"People walk and talk while sleepwalking all the time, don't they? And I'm sure you've heard of rarer instances of driving, cooking, eating. Well, the difference here is that half of the patient is consciously in control while the other is on autopilot. There are some personality changes, and reaction time does suffer, but it's within acceptable limits."

Ocan swallowed. "What about REM sleep?" Without dreams, people died, or at least went insane.

Weissman pressed her lips together. "Good question, and I'd be happy to answer if you sign onto the project—it's all classified at this point. Between Korea and Syria, we spend a billion dollars a year treating PTSD. If there's a way to cut that, even partially, it would represent a tremendous victory."

Ocan blinked. It made no sense. Patients should need more sleep to process the horror they'd been through, not less. Perhaps...

Ocan glanced up and realized several minutes passed while he daydreamed explanations. He went to apologize but stopped at the smug look on Weissman's face.

He was hooked, and she knew it.

***

The next eighteen months flew by in a storm of study design, approval and execution. Ocan oversaw the secret clinical trial, following 117 PTSD patients for 12 months. The results were better than he'd hoped: Nearly 80 percent of patients reported a significant reduction of PTSD symptoms.

He called his mother with the news, a first. They'd never talked about why he went into sleep disorders as his specialty, nor why his parents had fled their beloved, war-torn Uganda when he was just a baby.

"We all carry ghosts. You are a good son, to wish you could have made your father's easier to bear," his mother said quietly. Then she added, "But you work too much. Darianna says you don't even return her phone calls?"

Ocan stifled a sigh. His mother was always using his sister-in-law to try and check on him.

"I'm fine," he said tightly and ended the conversation as soon as he could. He didn't expect her to understand, what with her four children and six grandkids scattered across the United States and United Kingdom. Family was her everything, but work was all he had left.

So, he went all in. A few weeks later, when it was time to go public with the study's results, Major Weissman insisted Ocan handle all the interviews, even though she was the one who had developed the unisleep protocols.

"They'll trust a medical doctor more than a military scientist," she reasoned. "Plus, you're a professor over at Duke. That buys instant credibility."

He thought she was paranoid. Then the news hit.

The first week, the feeds went nuts, pumping out headlines like, "The End of Sleep" and "U.S. Government to Create Zombie Army." A week later, the mood shifted. Listicles touted the "Top 10 Reasons to Dream Like a Dolphin" and cheered the NASDAQ, which soared on speculation that unilateral sleep would allow people to work, shop or eat 24 hours a day.

Ocan smiled through such craziness. The science behind unisleep had existed for years, he explained to the public, and was just being used in a novel way.

"First, a neurotransmitter cocktail, originally developed to treat epilepsy, is injected into the patient. This quiets their corpus collosum, the part of the brain that helps the two halves communicate. Then, the patient sits under a magnetic brain stimulator, which sends out pulses to stimulate the right half to stay awake for three hours while the left sleeps. Then vice versa, followed by induced REM."

Of course, it was more complicated than that. But by then, his 30-second soundbite was up, and there was barely time to mention the next phase of research, an even larger, long-term study.

"This," he promised the pundits, "is just the beginning."

***

The weaver is naked, and the cobbler is barefoot.

It was an old saying of his grandfather's, and it never rang truer as another marathon workweek came to a close. Between all the media attention and his regular workload, Ocan couldn't remember when he'd last had a full night's sleep. So, thank God his last patient no-showed and he could leave early for the first time in a year.

He stood outside the hospital, about to climb into a car, when a woman called out.

"Doctor Kato!"

He pretended not to hear.

"Doctor Kato, please!"

He glanced up to see a woman dragging a sheepish-looking husband across the parking lot. Ocan sighed and signaled for the car to move on without him.

"Thanks for stopping," the woman huffed, breathless in a Southern accent. "I just wanted to say thank you."

Ocan couldn't place her. She had strawberry blonde hair and a sunburn across her nose. The man looked vaguely familiar, your average middle-aged white guy.

The man extended his palm. "Eric Adams. Sorry we're late for my follow-up. I gotta say, it's been like a miracle."

Adams. The Air Force vet who'd almost strangled his wife in his sleep.

"This is Jenny," Adams said.

"A pleasure," Ocan replied. His eyes flitted to her neck for a split second before he forced them back to her face.

"...it's just meant so much to us," she was saying. "Eric doesn't like to talk about how hard it was—me afraid, and him not trusting himself. But everything's changed."

She placed a hand over her belly, then reached out and gave Ocan a squeeze with the other. The gesture's meaning was obvious; she was pregnant. Adams wrapped an arm around her shoulder, chest swelling.

Ocan wavered, like a candle burning next to the sun, realizing how faint he flickered. Why had he wanted to go home early? There was nothing to go home to.

He forced a smile. "Congratulations." Then after an awkward pause, "Why don't you two come inside for the evaluation? No sense in making another trip just because you're a little late."

The wife hesitated. "It's not too much trouble?"

SportsCenter and greasy takeout–that's all he had to look forward to tonight. "No trouble at all."

And it wasn't. It took only thirty minutes for Ocan to complete the exam, enter everything into Adams' chart, and say goodbye.

All too soon, he stood alone under the sickly glow of the exam room's fluorescent lights. He'd dismissed the staff, and now the room was icy and silent. He stared at nothing.

Well, not nothing–at the 'dream machine,' as everyone now called it. Ocan slumped into the leather chair, over which the magnetic stimulator hung. The device–a helmet filled with magnetic coils–was originally designed to treat depression, but had fallen out of favor as cheaper, more effective drugs became available.

The dull ache in Ocan's chest eased as he pondered why the device worked so well for PTSD. One old study had documented the "first night effect"–people's tendency to sleep poorly on their first night in an unfamiliar place–and suggested that humans retained and occasionally used old, unilateral sleep pathways when they felt threatened or uneasy. It followed that PTSD patients felt uneasy all the time, so perhaps unilateral sleep was what their bodies craved.

But there was a catch. Ocan suspected humans had forgotten how to use these ancient pathways correctly. PTSD patients, left on their own, might routinely try and fail to enter unilateral sleep, never fully resting one side of the brain or the other. Worst of all, this would block REM sleep. The result: trauma lingered, even amplified, rather than fading with time.

Patients receiving the treatment, however, sustained periods of both unilateral and REM sleep. In fact, patients reported incredibly vivid dreams. Some described out of body experiences in which they relived battles, sometimes with far different outcomes, their terror replaced by peace or, at least, acceptance. Others swore they had conversations with lost loved ones, during which they were able to say goodbye, to let go.

Ocan's stomach twisted. To see Eimy again? What would he give for such a thing?

In answer, he lowered the device over his head and turned it on. Before he lost his nerve, he injected the neurotransmitter cocktail into his arm.

This was foolish. Stupid. But screw it. Everyone had gone home. He wanted to go home, too. *To her.*

A warm wave washed over him as the drug kicked in. The polysomnogram recorded the peaks and valleys that meant his brain had entered slow wave sleep. He smiled and reached for his laptop. He could do paperwork while he waited...

He smelled her first. It was the lotion she'd always used, shea butter scented with vanilla and cashmere extract. Then came her footsteps, soft on the linoleum. Followed by the tingle of her hand on his arm.

"Hey, baby," she murmured.

He opened his eyes, and the sweet pain of her pierced him as she gazed down. Those brown eyes. Those tight curls framing her face. And her smile, the gap between her teeth, where her pink tongue had always teased him as she spoke. She'd never known, and it had driven him crazy, even when they used to have their stupid little fights. Especially then.

"Hey," he replied, stirring. His throat was dry. It hurt to talk. To breathe. "I've missed you so much."

Then she was gone. Just like that, gone. A high-pitched ringing filled his ears. He winced, sat up and glanced around the frigid exam room.

Alone. Again.

***

Ocan groaned. "What do you mean they've asked for another revision?"

Three months in, and the long-term study threatened to go off the rails. First, he'd had trouble recruiting test subjects, who balked at coming into the hospital every other night for two years, no matter how promising the treatment. Then, his research budget was cut by 15 percent, thanks to the political geniuses in Congress.

And now, more headaches, curtesy of a bureaucratic tangle of institutional review boards. They couldn't even agree on the language to put in patient consent forms.

"Do I even want to know their reasoning?" he growled at the hospital staffer bearing the bad news. "Never mind. Just email it to me. I'll stay late and resubmit."

Then the phone rang. It was the secretary for the dean of Duke's College of Medicine, calling to say he'd missed their meeting. Again. Ocan cursed silently, apologized and promised to see the dean tomorrow. Then, glancing at the clock that said it was time to head home, he dove into the glut of final exams he needed to grade.

By the time he finished, the hospital wing was silent. He stood and stretched, walked out into the adjacent research lab, then peered into the neurodiagnostic clinic down the hall.

Empty. Finally. He headed to Exam Room 2, locking the door behind him.

It'd been a whole week since he'd used the device. That was the rule he made for himself: Only once a week, and only at night when no one was around. If he got caught–it was ridiculous, really, but a fact nonetheless–they would pull him from the trial.

Ocan slid into the chair and, heartbeat rising, pumped himself full of the drug. Then he turned the machine on and pulled the helmet over his head.

OK, so it wasn't ridiculous that someone might question the validity of his results if they knew he was using the device. In fact, he would have once done the same. But unisleep enabled him to get extra work done, work vital to keeping his head above water as his studies grew more complex. And then, during dreams, well, it was all so fascinating...

Each time he went under was different. Sometimes the dreams were just snippets of memory played like a movie on a screen. Other times, he glimpsed what seemed like alternative versions of the future, including ones in which Eimy never got sick: A trip to Hawaii they'd always talked about taking. A rained-out picnic by a lake he didn't recognize.

As he sat typing on his laptop, working on a proposal for an at-home machine that would make treatments more accessible, half his brain cycled through unisleep, then the other. But his fingers moved slower and slower. As the hours slipped by, the proposal didn't seem so important. Only one thing did.

And then, there she was.

She looked so young, wearing tattered jeans and her favorite T-shirt emblazoned with the red and blue of the Dominican flag. No makeup. She played with a delicate gold chain around her neck as her forehead furrowed.

"Hey baby," he whispered, voice thick, the words having become a kind of charm, a prayer, at the start of each session.

Then he watched himself walk into the room beside her.

"Hey, so I was wondering. What do you want for your birthday?" his young-self asked.

Ocan's stomach twisted at the memory, but he couldn't look away.

His wife shrugged as she gave an uneasy grin. "You'll think it's stupid."

"It's *your* birthday."

She peered down at her hands. "I want to get my eggs frozen."

His younger version faltered. "Is this about your sister?"

She scowled. "No." Then jutted out her chin. "What if it is?"

Her sister had been trying to get pregnant for forever. Low egg quality, the specialists said.

"She's only three years older," Eimy said. "What if, when we finally have the money and time to have a baby--"

"You're only turning 33." Plus, they'd barely been married a year, and she'd just gone back to school to get her master's in occupational therapy. "We have time."

260

"We don't know that. I've already done the research. There's a clinic only twenty minutes from here."

So she'd already decided. His younger self rolled his eyes. "Then why are we even having this conversation?"

"Because, I don't know, you're my husband?!" Her nostrils flared. "And hopefully, one day..." Her face crumpled as tears welled.

Ocan's younger self rushed to her side. "You're right." He took her into his arms. "I'm sorry. I'll go with you." And because she still held herself stiffly, he nuzzled her ear lobe.

It worked. She pulled him into a long kiss. When she came up for air, she gave a little smile and murmured, "In the meantime, we could start 'practicing' more."

***

"Hello, Dr. Kato? This is Melissa Polasky with *The Washington Times*. I'm calling about an article I'm working on, about Unisleep."

Ugh. Reporters. The more successful he became, the more they were an occupational hazard. Especially now that he headed the neurological research division for Foster Pharmaceuticals International.

Ocan forced cheer into his voice. "How can I help?"

Although he'd stunned colleagues at the hospital when he left two years ago at the end of his phase II clinical trial, he had no regrets. No more panels and politics, no more wrangling for grant money or enduring endless delays.

Instead, he possessed a large staff and an even larger research budget. Already, the company had taken his design for a portable unisleep machine and gotten it to market. Use of the device had exploded across the United States.

Of course, nothing was perfect, which was why the reporter was calling. As with the larger unisleep machine, there were some rare side effects: Dizziness, confusion, hallucinations. And, as with other popular treatments, some people abused it, which the media seized on for an easy story.

This time, the journalist explained, it was an 8-year-old boy from Texas.

"He was secretly using his father's device to stay up all night for months, playing video games. He started experiencing delusions in school--that he and his fellow students were all players trapped in the game. Later, his parents found him unconscious in his room. He'd drunk a bottle of Windex, convinced it was slurp juice, a healing potion from Fortnite."

Ocan shuddered. Poor kid. Poor stupid kid.

"Thankfully, the ER doctors saved him," the reporter continued. "Any comment?"

Ocan sighed. By now, he'd memorized his safety spiel.

"This technology treats insomnia and PTSD," he recited. "Although it is sometimes prescribed off-label for depression and minor parasomnia, it has not been approved for use in children. Patients with the device in their home must exercise adequate supervision of minors."

"Perfect," she said. "Thanks."

He sighed again and hung up. He'd always wanted to be a father, but he'd never really considered the thousand different ways you could screw it up. It wasn't hard to imagine himself, passed out after a hard day, his own child sneaking onto the computer. If he and Eimy had kids before she got sick, he'd be parenting all alone, and that boy in Texas could have easily been his.

So perhaps it was all for the best. Still...

Without realizing it, Ocan reached for the unisleep device hidden in the credenza to the right of his desk. He was using it more lately, ever since his dreams changed.

The first few times, the dreams had confused him. Instead of starting with the usual smell of vanilla and shea butter, they began with the sound of laughter. Then, one day, there she sat: A giggling toddler playing in a sand box at a nearby park.

"Time to go, *mija*," Eimy had called to the little girl in his dream. When she didn't respond, his wife had added, "I already gave you a five-minute warning, Dembe. Come on, Daddy's waiting."

Ocan's breath had caught. *Daddy?*

The next night, he dreamed of Eimy cheering from the sidelines of an indoor gym as their daughter, suddenly a preteen, played volleyball. A week later, an older version of himself–gray where he still had hair, a flabby pooch hanging over his belt–dropped an impossibly grownup version of the girl off at a brick-clad university.

He glanced at the clock on his office holoscreen. It was 3 p.m., too early to go home without raising eyebrows. But if he hooked himself up to the machine, the nice buzz that enveloped him during unisleep would improve an otherwise tedious afternoon of emails. By the time the dreams hit, everyone would have gone home. He could lock his office door, and, as usual, no one would be the–

A knock interrupted. His boss, Richard Zhou, poked his head in.

"Afternoon!" Rich was always unnaturally chipper, probably from all those zeros on the end of his salary. "I was just talking to Maria. She mentioned you were on the phone with a reporter?"

Really? Rich was checking up on his calls? Ocan hid his annoyance. "She just wanted a comment on a minor incident."

"You're too important to waste your time with that."

"Sure. Hey, did you see the Parkinson's study that came out yesterday?"

Rich shot him a look. "I'm serious. Run those calls through media relations. This comes from Myers."

Odd. The CEO never got involved. "What's happened?"

Rich's mouth pinched. "A lawsuit. We can't comment."

***

"So, what you're saying, Dr. Kato, is that your company doesn't actually know if your product is safe to use," the lawyer said.

Dear God, just put him out of his misery. The 8 a.m. deposition was supposed to take two hours, but they'd been sitting at this giant conference table for five.

"No." Ocan willed his voice even. "What I'm saying is we're still in trials."

"Trials? You've already sold tens of thousands of units for home use."

Careful. His lawyers warned him about this. Most people assumed all medical devices went through exhaustive testing.

"The technology is similar to those larger models used in hospitals. So we obtained expedited PMA from the FDA, contingent on post-approval studies."

"But that was over a year ago. When will the studies be complete?"

"That depends on recruitment and other—"

"Recruitment?" The lawyer's head swung like a bear catching scent of salmon. "You haven't started recruiting yet?"

Shit. "No, we're past that stage." Technically. A pool of patients waited somewhere in Asia, where research costs were cheaper. They just hadn't started testing yet.

"Good, then your attorneys won't mind our request for documents pertaining to..."

As the two sides argued, Ocan's mind churned. Forty-two people had died while using the portable unisleep machine. His lawyer assured him he had nothing to worry about. She said that because most of the cases were suicides, it would be near impossible to prove the device was the cause of death, rather than the underlying illness.

Still, Ocan felt like he'd swallowed something sharp and sour.

"You did well," the company lawyer told him when the deposition was over. "You stayed calm. That's the important thing."

"*That's* the important thing?" He snorted. Without waiting for her reply, he rose and headed home.

Sleep called to him as soon as he slammed the front door. The needle slid into his arm like silk. The scalp cap cradled his head like a pillow as he laid down on the couch. He closed his eyes, willing the hours to fade, waiting to hear his daughter's laugh.

Instead: A beeping. A piercing tone that stood his hair on end. He knew this memory, this room, too well.

Eimy lay in her hospital bed, a bandana covering her head. She'd pulled the covers up to her chin but still shivered.

"Hey baby." His voice broke.

"Come here," she beckoned, her hand splotched with bruises from too many IVs. "It's time to say goodbye."

He'd hated her for that. Hated and loved her. She was stronger than him, even until the end.

"I only have two regrets," she said. "One: never having a child. And two: that because of me, you might miss out. I know I have no right to tell you how to live once I'm gone, but I want you to marry again. Love someone."

"Shh." He crawled into bed with her, careful to avoid the morphine drip. "Don't talk like that. We're going to make it through this, together."

***

A few months after the lawsuit was filed, a judge dismissed it—although not because the product was safe. The ruling centered around a technical motion, something about suing in federal versus state court.

The company lawyers claimed a victory, then quietly advised Foster Pharmaceuticals that they had won a battle, not the war. Now that allegations had been made, the FDA would call for the post-approval studies sooner, rather than never, and the device would get a tougher review. In the meantime, ambulance chasers would lob legal grenades their way, probing for weakness.

Ocan wasn't sure how to feel. His mind buzzed. He went home early again. That's when he got the phone call.

"This is Mrs. Adams. Eric's wife."

Oh God, the widow. He'd been instructed to avoid contact with any plaintiffs, but Ocan remembered the praise she'd showered on him in the parking lot.

Now her voice dripped venom: "The lawyers just told us the news. That you can keep killing patients and there's nothing we can do about it. Congratulations."

When Ocan first saw her last name on the lawsuit, he couldn't help researching why. He'd learned her husband had a relapse. Jenny woke to him beating her with his service pistol. She'd begged him to stop, their young son asleep only a few feet away in the same bed.

He hadn't. When Adams finally came to, he thought she was dead. He called 911, told the operator he was sorry. Then he barred himself in his bathroom and shot himself.

Ocan reeled at the agony in Jenny's voice. It didn't seem possible he could feel both wrongly accused and remorseful at the same time, but there it was.

"Ma'am, I'm sorry for your loss. Your husband was a good man. But unisleep helped him for a long time."

"Yeah, in the hospital—until your trial ended, you disappeared, and the only other specialist who would see him had a seven-month wait for an appointment," she spat. "Did you know his symptoms returned? He thought it *his* fault, because supposedly 'everyone else' was cured."

"I didn't–"

"His doctor eventually wrote him a script for your home kit. It didn't work well, but now it's all insurance will cover. So, he started using it more and more and then..."

Ocan shook his head. "I'm sorry, but those decisions weren't made by my company. We are very careful to–"

"To cover your asses, yes. Imply one thing in your commercials with smiling faces and inspirational music, then mutter a bunch of horrible side effects that you think no one will notice. And, why not? Because the politicians let you get away with it, your hands stuffed so far up their--"

Enough. "Mrs. Adams, I understand you need someone to blame. But this device has helped thousands of people. The law is on our side."

"He was your patient, once." Her voice cracked. "*You're* supposed to be on his side."

***

Someone pounded on the front door. But if Ocan ignored them, they'd go away. Same with phone calls and texts, like little birds. They'd sing and sing, but eventually settle down in their nests for the night.

Boom-boom-boom-boom-boom.

This person was persistent. How nice of them. How annoying. It was probably Rich, wondering why he hadn't come to work in a week. Or was it two?

Boom-boom-boom.

Maybe it was his mother. No, he hadn't told her anything. She was busy enough, retired from nursing but practically running the Ugandan American Community Center in Waltham now. Last thing she needed was—

Boom-boom-buh-BAM!

The front door flung open. Ocan half expected to see a burly police officer kicking it in. Instead, his tiny sister-in-law barreled forward.

A dream? These days, it was getting harder to tell.

"Darianna." His voice croaked from disuse.

She turned to him on the couch. Her eyes widened as she cursed, "*Coño.*"

She made him take a shower, laid out some clean clothes. She shaved off his beard, which shook him from his stupor.

"Why are you here?" he asked as she stood in the kitchen, making him a ham and swiss cheese sandwich with groceries she'd brought. "Seriously. You don't need--"

"Shut up." She pointed the butter knife at him. "Shut. Up."

"Fine." He gritted his teeth. He hadn't heard from her in months, since he'd stopped answering her phone messages that she was 'just checking in.'

They didn't talk for a while. Turned out the ham sandwich she'd made was for her. The next one, his, was turkey. She remembered he didn't eat pork. His face grew hot as they ate in silence.

"I'm sorry," he finally blurted. "I...thank you."

"You're welcome."

"Dari—"

"You don't need to pretend."

"You heard about the lawsuit? Don't worry. We won." Bitterness filled his voice.

She frowned. "This isn't about the lawsuit." Her eyes wandered to the living room, where the unisleep machine sat on a side table. She walked over and inspected it, almost reverently.

"You know everyone is using this now," she murmured. "Poor people who need to work double, triple shifts. Executives scheming to get ahead. But mostly, it's the dreams everyone likes. The dreams that keep everyone coming back."

Ocan stared, horror spreading across his face.

She gave a small, sad shrug. "I can see the appeal. Who wants to walk through this world totally awake? Who wouldn't love to live in a fantasy of their own making?"

She put the device down and looked out the window. From the way she crossed her arms, wrapping them around her middle as if holding in a wound, he knew she wasn't talking about him. Or even Eimy. She was thinking about the children she would never have.

She turned and glared at him, fierce as an eagle.

"I'm not asking you to forget Eimy," she said. "All I'm asking is for you to see: Whatever life we have, it's one she didn't get. So do something to deserve it. Hiding behind this?"—she held up the device—"It's disgusting."

***

Darianna was right. He told himself he'd do it only one more time. To say goodbye.

He did everything as usual. He waited through both unilateral cycles, then waited some more. But it seemed stuck. Had his sister-in-law sabotaged the machine? How dare—

"Hi Daddy."

His daughter stood smiling. She looked about 6, clinging to a raggedy stuffed penguin.

"Uh, hi, honey," he answered. He looked around the dream. "Have you seen your mother?"

Her eyes flew wide and her mouth made a surprised "o," then quivered as tears threatened. "That's not a very nice thing to ask."

"Why?"

She screwed up her face, about to bawl, then stuck out her chin in an expression of defiance so like her mother, his chest hurt.

"Tell me about how you made me, Daddy," she said. "How you made me special."

His skin prickled. "What?"

"Rose at school says her mommy carried her in her tummy for nine months. I told her Mamá died before I was born. Rose wanted to know how I got here. But I couldn't remember it all."

Ocan's breath stuttered, but his daughter continued:

"I'm glad Tia Darianna carried me in her tummy, since Mamá couldn't. But how did Mamá put me in there?"

***

Ocan didn't waste any time when he returned to work. He called a meeting with Rich and Meyers and stalked into the executive office.

"We have to pull Unisleep from the market," he said as the two men stood to greet him.

Rich's jaw dropped, but the CEO appraised him with amusement, almost as if he hadn't spoken. "Welcome back," Meyers said. "How was your vacation?"

When Ocan didn't answer, Rich edged between them with an uneasy grin. "Don't let that lawsuit get to you. It's over."

Bullshit. Just this morning, there was a newsfeed about another death, yet another widow he'd created. "This isn't about lawsuits," Ocan said. "It's about what's right for patients."

Meyers rolled his eyes.

Ocan pushed on: "We need to do studies–long-term studies–on side effects. We need to educate physicians, so it doesn't end up in the wrong hands."

Meyers face hardened. "What's happened to you, son? This is your baby, and here you are, reacting out of fear. You're supposed to be a man of science."

"The science was never completed," Ocan said. "You know that better than anyone. And by the time it is, it'll be too late. They'll all be addicted."

"Addicted?" Mock surprise crossed Meyers' face. "And how would *you* know that?"

The threat lay there between them, writhing like a snake. They knew about his habit. They'd always known. And now, so did he, with utter certainty: The company would never pull the product, never give an inch. He'd been half-asleep for two years, and if he took his concerns public, they'd ruin him.

Meyers' smile spread like oil. "Look, there's no need for all this. You're overworked. Take another few weeks off, get your head straight. When you come back, everything will be waiting. Your salary, your position—or a new one, if you like. We have an opening in senior management. Less work, more money. How's that sound?"

As Meyers spoke, he wheeled out a unisleep machine, the updated version, smaller and sleek. Ocan stared. Did the old bastard really think that was going to work?

Yet, his mind itched for it. Despite everything, the thing he wanted most was to lie down and hook himself up. To be with Eimy and their daughter.

And, with that thought, finally, he understood. There was only one way he could make at least part of his dream come true.

***

Ocan stared at the linoleum floor of the hospital waiting room. A line of green tiles led to surgery, a magenta stripe to maternity, and yellow to the emergency room.

So many paths to choose from. Had he taken the right one? He turned his gaze from the lines on the floor to those on his palms and muttered, "The program works if you work it."

It was a stupid saying the counselors had recited at his first unisleep addiction meeting, a motto he'd immediately hated. It was trite, clichéd, and—to his chagrin and eternal gratitude—also true. He hadn't used the device in well over a year.

Still, his hands shook. An echo of old symptoms or just nerves? Either was understandable, considering that after he quit Foster Pharmaceuticals and went public about the device, the company launched a smear campaign and sued him for disclosure of trade secrets. Now no research institution would touch him.

"Dr. Kato, they're ready to see you."

Ocan shot to his feet as he turned toward the nurse. He flew down the hospital corridor, following the magenta line, but when he reached the doorway, he faltered.

Inside, his sister-in-law beckoned. She lay in the hospital bed, her dark hair slick with sweat. She beamed. "Well, come on now, come hold her."

He rushed forward to cradle his daughter. She was teeny, head pointy from the birth canal. She took one look at him and screamed.

"Just like her mama," he chuckled. Then, with a glance at his sister-in-law, he quickly amended, "Both her mamas."

Darianna laughed, loud and easy.

"Sounds like a party," her husband called as he bustled into the room. Mauricio carried a brown bag from a local bakery and a stuffed penguin, behind which trailed five pink balloons. He pecked his wife on the cheek and, with a flourish from the bag, presented her with a golden empanadita dulce dusted with powdered sugar.

"Ask, and ye shall receive," he boomed.

"A-men," Darianna said, holding Ocan's gaze.

Ocan marveled at her, hoping both she and Mauricio would one day take him up on his other offer, if they wanted it: Eimy's last gift.

With an outstretched finger, he caressed his little girl's cheeks, traced her shoulders, wrinkled toes. Already, she had Eimy's large eyes and his long, skinny feet.

Oh God, what was he thinking? He was going to ruin her. He'd spent an hour installing that damn car seat, but it was still all wobbly. He was too old for this, 41, for God's sake.

And too broke. After the scandal, he had to start his psychiatry practice all over in a dingy little shopping center on the rough side of town. True, it had been gratifying when the FDA finally finished its investigation, issued a recall, and Foster Pharmaceuticals' stock plummeted. Still, between legal fees, insurance and Darianna's IVF treatments, he'd barely made payroll this month. So how would he save for college?

"Breathe," his sister-in-law murmured, catching his look of panic. "All we have to do is show her we love her. You just stay in the present. The future will take care of itself."

The present, yes. Here he would stay. No more reliving the past and regretting a lost future. Instead, he would make a new one. He snuggled his daughter close and smiled.

"Hey baby."

Seven Strands

Tisha Marie Reichle-Aguilera

Chicana Feminist and former Rodeo
Queen, Tisha Marie Reichle-Aguilera
(she/her) writes so the desert landscape
of her childhood can be heard as loudly
as the urban chaos of her adulthood.
She is obsessed with food. A former
high school teacher, she earned an
MFA at Antioch University Los
Angeles and is an Annenberg Fellow at
University of Southern California. She
is a Macondista and works for literary
equity through Women Who Submit.
You can read her other stories and essays
at http://tishareichle.com/

"It's real churchy in here." Norma touched the foot of the cruci-fied Jesus. "When did your mom become so religious?"

Cristian answered, "Mi tía's been here all week. Clearly she has redecorated."

They maneuvered around the large couch and chair, put their suitcases in the corner by the row of burning candles: one giant Virgen de Guadalupe, two sacred hearts, and three smaller saints Norma didn't recognize. "Last time we were here —"

"Last time," Cristian snapped, "my mom wasn't sick."

Norma raised her eyebrows. Cristian was more upset than he had let on while they were driving out here. His incessant chat-ter about Dodger statistics was normal. But so was his silence as they exited the freeway on the outskirts of town, two exits before the one where his mom lived. He'd said he needed to drive along the rural roads to prepare mentally for his return. He'd always felt like some kind of transformation was necessary to be the son she expected. Norma didn't have the power to conjure that kind of change.

They were greeted at the door by a shorter, wider version of Cristian's mom whose voice was higher. "There you are, precioso de mi vida." She spoke so fast, Norma had to adjust to listen. "Lemme look atchoo. Too flaco. Doesn't that girlfriend of yours feed you? Lemme make you a plate."

Norma touched her arms, worried she was invisible, and looked around to see if they'd travelled back to 1950.

"Tia, this is Norma. And she doesn't have to feed me. I'm thirty-two. I can feed myself."

Magdalena ignored Norma's outstretched hand and smoothed nonexistent wrinkles out of Cristian's shirt.

He maneuvered out of her clutches. "Whatever you're cooking smells delicious."

"Sit. Sit." Magdalena moved her bag of yarn off the kitchen table and patted the seat. Just one seat.

"I'd like to see my mom first."

"I'd like to use the baño," Norma muttered in his ear.

"Si. Si. She's been waiting for you all week, mi'jo. We thought you'd be home sooner."

"I had to work, Tia. What did the doctor say?"

"She's been feeling worse every day. Chela gave her some hierba buena the first two days but that didn't help."

"Is Chela the local doctor?" Norma asked.

Magdalena scowled at her.

"Tia, what happened when you took my mom to the doctor yesterday?"

Magdalena waved his question away before she opened the door and whispered. "She has been sleeping so much. But she's been waiting for you. We thought you'd come sooner."

The room was dark when they entered. Only a tiny crack of light slipped through the opening in the heavy green drapes. The menthol and stale breath caught Norma off guard. She started choking, coughed to cover her discomfort.

"Shhh! I told you she was sleeping," Magdalena hissed at Norma and pushed her toward the doorway.

"Magdalena, ya. I'm awake. I've been awake for a while, I think. But it's difficult to tell in this darkness." Cristian's mom lifted herself up to a half-seated position and sneezed. "Open a window or something. I thought I was already in the tomb."

Cristian obeyed. The sunlight revealed his mom, thin and pale under a mountain of heavy quilts.

Maybe Magdalena was trying to smother her to death. Norma narrowed her eyes at Magdalena's back. That'd make Cristian extra guilty. If she'd died before they could drive over to see her. Then he'd be indebted to his Tia forever.

"Norma, mi'ja, so glad you're here." Cristian's mom patted the edge of the bed next to her. "Cristian tells me you're starting law school in the fall. Que bueno." She beckoned Norma from the doorway. "Come in. Is Cristian taking good care of you?"

"I take care of myself most of the time."

"Ah, of course you do. That's why I like you mi'ja."

Magdalena made a disapproving noise in her throat.

"Ignore my sister. 'Sta loca."

Magdalena scowled and stomped out of the room. They could hear her banging pots in the kitchen.

Cristian stood on the other side of his mom, took her hand in his. "What did the doctor say?"

"Que doctor? That quack Ramirez? He'd probably tell me I need surgery or give me a bottle of some drug no one ever heard of. I go to him, I die for sure." She turned to Norma, "My sister wants to die first, so she can be the center of everyone's attention."

"Mom!" Cristian knelt at his mom's bedside. "You're not— dying, are you? Is that what the doctor said?"

"What doctor? Your Tia had her neighbor, Chela, come over here and burn stuff and make me tea and rub smelly stuff on me while they chanted prayers in Spanish and some other language I didn't understand."

Norma looked around the room for anything this curandera, Chela, might have left behind, objects that might impede her progress with Magdalena. She fingered the red candle on the nightstand. The wax was cool but still soft, so she took some under her pinky and thumb nails.

Cristian asked, "So you've had no medical care?"

"When my sister left to the store, I hopped into the kitchen and made an ice pack for my ankle. I told her I could take care of myself. Like you, Norma, I'm independent. But she insisted on staying here all week, insisted on telling you to come here." She patted Cristian's hand. "I am glad to see you." She looked up at Norma. "Both of you."

"Your ankle, Mom?"

"It hurts more than my knee."

"Knee? Mom, what exactly happened?"

"I fell coming up the front steps in a hurry to answer the phone. I was carrying too many grocery bags, like I always do, and I lost my balance. Ni modo. The swelling's already gone down. I've kept it elevated like they say on the WebMD."

"Tia made it seem like you had some kind of episode, a heart attack or a stroke or something. She said you couldn't talk to me because—"

"Ay, Magdalena has always been mucha exagerada. You know that."

Norma held in her chuckle. Cristian had been in agony all week, worried his mom would die before he could take days off work and make the four-hour drive east to Blythe.

"I did not know that!" He walked to the bedroom doorway. "Tia!"

Norma had not seen him this angry since the Lakers last losing season.

"Tia, get in here!"

"No seas tan malcriado, Cristian." His mom turned to Norma, "My sister tends to be how the kids say today, duh-ra-muh!"

Norma let out her laughter.

"It's not funny, Norma!" Cristian paced the floor at the foot of the bed. "All this time, Tia had me believing—"

"You believe what you want, chamaco." Magdalena appeared in the doorway with a different tone. "All I said was your mom needed you. You needed to be here. That's what sons are for."

Before Cristian could explode at Magdalena, Norma stood up and stepped between them. "That's why we're here. To see what his mom needs." She walked closer to Magdalena, eyes opened extra wide, maintained her calm tone. "Maybe what they need is a few moments alone." As she stepped forward, Magdalena stepped backward into the hall. "I'd love to see what you are making with that bright green yarn out there." She closed the bedroom door behind her. "As soon as I go to the bathroom."

Magdalena continued walking backward all the way to the kitchen, clearly mesmerized by Norma. "Would, would you like some tea?"

"Tea. Yes. Gracias, Tia." Norma held Magdalena's gaze until Magdalena was forced to look away and fill the tea kettle with water. This was going to be easier than Norma thought.

In the bathroom, she put the wax scrapings on to a square of toilet paper. She splashed water on her face and stared at her dripping reflection. The outward pattern said it would take a minor spell to convert Magdalena. Cristian's mom had been much more of a challenge when they had met last year, and now she knows Norma is what's best for her son. Norma rummaged through the bag on the counter and pulled seven strands of Magdalena's bright red hair from a jeweled clip. She pulled seven strands of her own from the nape of her neck. She wrapped them together in the square of toilet paper with the red wax and put them in her pocket. In the drawer, she found the cream she knew Cristian's mom used nightly. She dabbed a bit behind each ear, just enough to confuse Magdalena.

In the living room, Norma blew out the saint candles and exhaled the smoke away with one hard breath. "Allergies," she said when Magdalena looked at her questioningly. She sat on the sofa next to Magdalena and pulled the coffee table closer so she could reach her tea.

Magdalena opened her yarn bag and explained the intricate stitches and patterns.

With her not drinking hand, Norma fingered the design, murmured what she hoped sounded like encouragement. She blew gently on her tea to cool it, sipped, aware that it was the same concoction Chela had given Cristian's mom. So she stealthily spit it back into her mug. "Still too hot," she said to Magdalena's curious gaze.

"Do you knit?" Magdalena asked. "Crochet?"

"Mi abuela taught me. Want my help?" Without waiting for a response, Norma took the needles from Magdalena and hummed a spell as she replicated the pattern Magdalena established.

Magdalena got out two smaller needles and started a new piece with a lighter shade of green.

"These two will look beautiful together."

Magdalena smiled and joined Norma in her humming.

When the tea was cold, Norma knew its potency was reduces. She opened her throat and gulped it all.

"Would you like some more?"

"Water would be fine, Tia."

When Magdalena got up, Norma removed the square of toilet paper from her pocket and stretched the seven strands of her hair and Magdalena's along the length of green yarn. She rubbed it all with a bit of wax to hold it together and quickly knitted their hair into the pattern. She twisted the yarn so her light brown and Magdalena's red hairs weren't visible at a glance.

Magdalena returned with two clear glasses of iced water.

Norma held hers up. "Salud." She stared through the glass at Magdalena's blurred reflection and watched as her hex took effect.

THANK YOU TO OUR SUPPORTERS

Many thanks to our patrons and supporters, especially:

Wichael Tellez • Cathrin Hagey
Natalie Weizenbaum • Kate Boyes
Johanna Levene

Alina Kanaski • Jeffery Reynolds • Myz Lilith
D.M. Domosea • carol shoemake • Erik DeBill
Frederick Stark • Bonnie Warford • Felicia OSullivan
Salomao Becker • Anna O'Brien • Martin Cohen
J'nae Spano • Tory Hoke • S Klotz

Ana Wang • Lorna D Keach • smokestack • Lisa Short
Sian Jones • Kristina Saccone • Rocky B • BethOfAus • J.
Askew • Dirck de Lint • Brit Hvide • Wanda • Karen Anderson
Charlotte Nash-Stewart • Liz Warner • Suzanne Thackston
Jen G • Emily Anderson • Maria Haskins • GriffinFire
Matthew Bennardo • Kayla

Want to see your name here? Become a patron!
patreon.com/lunastation

About the Cover Artist

My name is Theodora Daniela Capăt. I was born in 1989 in Bucharest, Romania. Currently I live in Vaxholm, Sweden.

In 2010 until 2013 I studied at The Swedish Academy of Realist Art SARA.

After my graduation I started working as a primary teacher at SARA and still do until this day. I have also worked as an intern at EA DICE Stockholm during summer of 2012. I am also two times winner for The America Portrait Society 2014 Certificate of Excellency and 2015 Exceptional Merit

www.capat.art

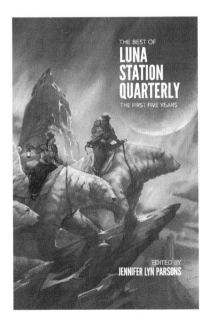